CRAZY, STUPID, DEAD

Also by Wendy Delaney

The Working Stiffs Mystery Series

CRAZY, STUPID, DEAD

A WORKING STIFFS MYSTERY

BOOK 7

Wendy Delaney

Sugarbaker Press

Sugarbaker Press
PO Box 3271
Redmond, WA 98073-3271

This is a work of fiction. Names, characters, places, and incidents are a product of the author's imagination. Locales and public names are sometimes used for atmospheric purposes. Any resemblance to actual people, living or dead, or to businesses, companies, events, institutions, or locales is completely coincidental.

Cover by Lewellen Designs

Printed in the United States of America

Crazy, Stupid, Dead/Wendy Delaney – 1st edition, November 2019

ISBN: 978-0-9986597-3-2

For Dad
Duke wouldn't be "the Duke" without you.

Acknowledgments

Like one of the characters in this story, I started to think that my "baby," *Crazy, Stupid, Dead*, might never be born. But after a few labor pains and the kind assistance of some special people in my life, Working Stiffs Mystery #7 was able to make its way into the world.

Kathy Coatney and Jody Sherin, you were instrumental in the idea stage. Thank you for lending me your brains and for being just an email away whenever I needed you.

Thanks as always to my resident "guy," Jeff—my Mr. Fix-it, who I go to for expert advice.

To "K," my "cop stuff" advisor, I'm so appreciative of the timely and thoughtful assistance you provide me. Steve, who needs to sound like a police detective, thanks you too!

Bonnie Terry, thanks for letting me borrow your name.

Elizabeth Flynn, fab sock diva and editor extraordinaire, I can't thank you enough for squeezing me into your busy schedule.

Lastly, I offer my heartfelt thanks to my dream team of beta-readers and supporters: Diane Garland, Heather Chargualaf, Deidre Herzog, Cindy Nelson, Lori Dubiel, Susan Cambra, Christie Marks, Brandy Lanfair-Jones, Kimber Hungerman, Amber Lassig, Connie Lightner, DeAnna Shaikoski, Vicki Huskey, Brenda Randolph, Donna Peterson, Jan Dobbins, Beth Rosin, Kath Maches, Barb Harland, Rebecca Reitze, Beth Carpenter, Renee Arthur, and Karen Haverkate. And thank you, Team Delaney! You all rock, and I'm very grateful to have you with me on my writing journey.

Chapter One

I should have known that Florence wouldn't have everything ready to go," my grandmother whispered to me the second that Florence Spooner disappeared into a back room of her condominium. "Since day one of her taking over as garden club president, it's been a disorganized disaster."

This wasn't the first time that Gram had groused about her fellow gardening enthusiast's shortcomings. "Then maybe you should have stayed on as president."

"And get stuck with that job for a sixth year in a row?" Gram shook her head, her helmet of spun-sugar curls not budging a millimeter. "No, when I turned eighty last year, I took a good look at everything I want to do before I leave this world, and serving another decade on the board wasn't on my list."

"Then how come you're the one who's taking over as secretary? Again," I added since I remembered my grandfather referring to her as "Madam Secretary" back when I was in high school.

Gram heaved a sigh. "Because I made the mistake of

letting Florence talk me into it after Naomi's funeral service."

"You need to learn how to say no."

"Ain't that the truth." Gram scowled past me at the top of the stack of white banker boxes labeled GARDEN CLUB in orange block letters. "You would think that, in this computer age, we could come up with a better system of maintaining historical records than stuffing paper into boxes."

Having worked in the Chimacam County Prosecutor's office for the last fourteen months, I couldn't agree more because we definitely featured an overabundance of paper historical records. Unfortunately, electronic solutions often required funds that would bust most rural counties' budgets. That left me as the lowly administrative assistant whose duty it was to stuff paper into boxes—in my case, a couple dozen metal file "boxes" that bordered the windowless beige walls surrounding my desk.

"At least there are only three boxes," I said, my ears detecting the whir of a laser printer coming to life. "Unless she's back there trying to fill up another one."

"Naomi passed a couple of days after the last board meeting, so I imagine Florence is making sure the records are up to date. Although why she couldn't have done that *before* we arrived, I don't have a clue."

There was no point in my standing there like a lump when I had a lunch date with my boyfriend after I fulfilled my pack mule duties, so this mule was motivated to get a move on. I picked up the top box and headed for the front door. "While she's finishing up, I'll take this to the car."

Gram opened the door for me. "We parked so far away. Are you sure you don't want to pull the car into the driveway first? I know that's heavy."

"It's not *that* heavy." Just as the words came out of my mouth the contents shifted, propelling me forward.

"Charmaine Digby," Gram called after me, using the parental tone that used to signal that I was in deep doo-doo. "I'll never forgive myself if you spend the rest of the weekend in traction because I asked for your help."

I glanced back over my shoulder. "Not to worry." I sucked in a deep breath, my flabby arm muscles screaming for oxygen. "I'll be back in a jiffy."

Back with the car that I could have sworn had been located a heckuva lot closer when I left it in the visitor parking area a few doors down.

"About time you got here," an elderly man buttoned up in a tweedy cardigan said, quickening his pace as he approached.

My pounding heart didn't need a sudden injection of adrenaline to kick it into high gear. Fortunately, I didn't sense danger because short of tossing the box like a shot put at the old dude, I had no way to defend myself.

Huffing and puffing the last ten feet to my grandmother's SUV, I balanced a corner of the box on the bumper while I fumbled with the tailgate latch. "I think ...you have me...confused with someone else."

He stepped up beside me. "Allow me to be of assistance, Miz Charmaine."

I stared at the diminutive man with the steel wool

hair and watched with some trepidation as he effortlessly popped the latch. Because I didn't know him, but he seemed to know me.

Frowning, he helped me load the box into the back of the SUV. "Child, what do you have in here, rocks?"

"No, it's—" It was none of his business. While the grandmother who raised me had trained me to be kind to my elders, she also valued her privacy. At least what little privacy she could carve out in a small coastal community dominated by a senior set fueled by local gossip. And since she wasn't the least bit pleased to be collecting stacks of club newsletters instead of digging in a flower bed on this sunny October Saturday, I opted in favor of an evasive answer. "Actually, I don't know. It's not—"

"Yours?" He nodded. "I know. I saw them move the boxes out of Naomi's place last week. You taking this one in as evidence?"

"Evidence?" Of what?

"I can't imagine you'll find anything very elucidatin' in there. At least the police weren't much interested in those old boxes when they processed the scene."

I still didn't know who this octogenarian was, other than the obvious—that he had been acquainted with the late Naomi Easley. But from his pattern of speech, he sounded like a transplant from the Deep South.

He gave me a hard look that I suspected had been intended to mirror the way I was staring. "Isn't that what you and your *friend*, Detective Sixkiller, call it? Processin' the scene?"

Okay, I couldn't take it anymore. "I'm sorry. Have we

met before?" Because he couldn't have made it more clear that he knew that Steve Sixkiller and I were a couple.

The man's expression softened, a smile dancing at his thin lips. "Miz Charmaine, I know it's been a few years, but don't be a heartbreaker and tell me that you don't remember me."

Crap. That was exactly what I was going to have to tell him if he didn't offer up something to clue me in.

"I'd have the Reuben with extra sauce on the side, and Jerome would have the tuna melt on..."

"Sourdough," we said in unison.

While I remembered the lunch order the southern gentlemen never varied from when they came to Port Merritt to visit family, I didn't recognize the lines of the kindly face looking at me, nor did I have a name to go with it.

I extended my limp noodle of an arm and shook his hand. "It's been more than a few years." Because I was probably nineteen and still working summers at my great-uncle Duke's diner the last time our paths crossed. "Mr...."

"Armistead." His watery blue eyes twinkled with good humor. "I'll say that you haven't changed a bit if you'll do the same for me."

Since I sported a thicker middle from eating my way through a divorce, and my jeans were doing nothing to conceal the saddlebags that had attached themselves to my thighs, he had a deal. "You got it, Mr. Armistead."

"Leland, please. We're old friends."

Not really, but I could go along with that, too. Plus, I wasn't picking up any nonverbal cues to cause concern. Except for the fact that this "old friend" clearly wanted something from me.

He inched closer. "So you can tell me. You don't believe Naomi's drownin' was just an accident, do you?"

Despite just having worked up a sweat by walking a hundred yards, an icy shiver went down my spine. "I don't have any reason to question the coroner's findings." And even if I did, since the Chimacam County Prosecutor/Coroner was my boss, I'd be committing career suicide to offer an unsolicited opinion.

"And yet, here you are at the scene of the crime," Leland said, thumbing in the direction of the for-sale sign stationed in front of the condo across the street. "Like my daddy used to say, 'It's not a coincidence when you turn up where you're supposed to be.'"

True, but I was going to be on the receiving end of an earful from my grandmother if I didn't turn up on Florence's doorstep in the next sixty seconds. "Sorry. I'm on a bit of tight schedule, so I wonder if we could continue this conversation another time."

He patted my hand. "I get it. You're not at liberty to divulge any information while you're conductin' an investigation."

I didn't know whether to thank Leland or set him straight. No coroner's investigation, open or closed, had ever existed to determine the manner of Naomi Easley's death. Since she'd obviously made the deadly decision to mix painkillers and alcohol before being found submerged in her bathtub, it hadn't been deemed necessary. "I—"

"And I know these things take time, but I am at your service anytime you'd like me to make a statement. I'm sure Mavis feels the same way."

I had no idea who he was talking about. "I'm sorry. Who's Mavis?"

"Lives across the street." Leland pointed at the mani-cured duplex in front of Gram's car. "She had a key to Naomi's house, so I got her to open the door when I couldn't reach her by phone. That's when Mavis discov-ered her cold as a mackerel in the tub, and I called the police to report the murder."

Murder?!

Chapter Two

"Leland Armistead clearly doesn't think Mrs. Easley's drowning was accidental," I said, laboring to keep up with Steve's long strides after the door of the Roadkill Grill closed behind us.

He turned to me as I crawled into the cab of his Ford pickup. "Mr. Armistead's entitled to his opinion. As is anyone else in town who would like to second-guess the opinion of the detective in charge of the investigation, and the coroner who carefully reviewed his report."

"I'm sure it was a very thorough report." Knowing Steve, painstakingly thorough.

"Then why are we having the same conversation we had three weeks ago?"

"Because drowning in your bathtub seems like a stupid way to die."

"It's not the smartest." Steve started the truck. "Goes to show how washing down prescription painkillers with a bottle of wine can be a deadly idea."

True. And that bit of wisdom should have been common knowledge after all the media attention that accompanied certain celebrity deaths. But...

"You're stating that like that's conclusive. Have you seen some toxicology results that I don't know about?" Because when I had made copies of Naomi Easley's death certificate for her family, the cause of death had not changed from the original *Undetermined, pending Toxicology.*

"Nope, too soon to get the report back from the crime lab, but I saw a couple of empty bottles next to the tub," Steve said, pulling out of the parking lot. "And since Mr. Armistead agreed with the family members that Naomi Easley was someone who drank wine on a regular basis, with no signs of a struggle, it appeared that she did some serious self-medicating. Probably passed out and slipped under the surface of the water."

I didn't have any reason to doubt Steve's professional opinion, especially since Frankie Rickard, the Chimacam County Prosecutor/Coroner, the elected official who had declined pursuing anything beyond a standard death investigation, had agreed with his assessment. "I'm sure you're right."

Steve shot me a sideways glance. "Now that wasn't so hard to say, was it?"

"Hey, it's not like I'm trying to argue Mr. Armistead's case for him. It's just a weird way for someone to go."

"I know. I saw something similar when I worked Homicide in Seattle. A guy a little older than us was found in his hot tub after a night of partying."

Okay, so Naomi Easley's death wasn't especially unique. "But that was a homicide?"

"Nope. Based on the autopsy results, cause of death was accidental drowning, but his blood alcohol level of point two something had a lot to do with it."

No doubt it had everything to do with it, but drowning in a hot tub seemed a heckuva lot more plausible than a bathtub. I was about to say so when my cell phone dinged with a text message.

Expecting news that my very pregnant best friend, Roxanne Fiske, had finally gone into labor, I pounced on my phone.

"Oh," I said with a sigh, reading the message from my actress mother's newest husband.

Heading over with something your mother wants you to have. You home?

After I responded that we were on our way there now, I turned to Steve. "Barry's on his way over with something."

"Again?"

In the five weeks since I had moved into Barry Ferris's rental house, hardly a weekend went by that I didn't see him arrive with some piece of furniture that my mother wouldn't allow him to keep in their new home.

"Again. I'm sure he won't stay long." Just long enough to ensure that my chow mix, Fozzie, hadn't scratched up the recently refinished hardwood floors.

"Any clue what it is this time?"

"Nada." Fortunately, I hadn't moved in with much furniture of my own, so Barry's hand-me-downs weren't entirely unwelcome.

Fifteen minutes later, my canine home alarm system alerted Steve and me to the high school teacher in his mid-fifties climbing out of his recently acquired Dodge pickup.

Waving as I followed Steve out the front door, my eyes zeroed in on the black behemoth strapped to the corners of the truck's bed. "What is that?" And why the heck was it showing up at my house like an oversized pigeon come home to roost?

"An elliptical machine," Barry said, injecting enough attitude into his voice to make it clear that he wasn't happy that "Mom" had forced him to return one of his toys.

Steve stepped to the tailgate and started untying one of the back straps. "Looks like a nice one. I assume the missus would prefer one that will make her a latte while she pedals."

All too aware of my mother's champagne taste, I thought Steve had to be hitting pretty close to the mark with that assumption.

Squinting against the glare of the midday sun, Barry grabbed the strap on his side like he wanted to choke someone with it. "It squeaks."

"Probably just needs a little lubrication," Steve stated as gently as if he were diffusing a bomb.

"Probably." Barry aimed that squint at me. "Only your mother decided that she needed to replace all the *outdated* equipment in the bedroom that she converted into a home gym. So the exercise bike is coming back, too."

A new million-dollar house, a new pickup, and now a

completely new home gym—all major expenditures made by a Hollywood actress accustomed to having money. But that lucrative income had existed before she had fallen off the B-list and borrowed against the house in the Santa Monica hills that she'd been trying to sell for most of the last year.

"I don't like the sound of that. Er... the spending, not the squeak." Because my mother appeared to be rolling the dice that her big-budget movie premiering next week would revitalize her floundering career.

Although I didn't mind the idea of getting a free exercise bike.

Barry didn't respond. He didn't have to. I could see the worry pulling at the corners of his mouth.

As Gram had bemoaned to me on several occasions, my former biology teacher had gotten a lot more than he'd bargained for with this marriage. But I'd had enough experience living through my mother's first three marriages to know that this wasn't something I wanted to get in the middle of.

With nothing left to say, I excused myself to put Fozzie in the backyard and then held the front door open for the men angling the piece of heavy equipment toward what had been an empty spare bedroom.

Barry winced as he dropped his side down with more force than I was sure he intended. "That's gonna leave a mark," he said, his eyes tracking two dog-hair dust bunnies tumbling toward the doorway.

When he met my gaze I felt as guilty as when he caught me chewing gum in class twenty years back, and I made a quick exit to fetch a broom. "I was just about to do some housework when Steve stopped by to take me to lunch."

"Sure you were," Steve whispered as he followed me down the hall.

"Shhh, I don't need my landlord to think that he made a big mistake when he rented me this house."

"Trust me, that's not the mistake he's thinking about right now."

Grabbing a broom from the laundry room, I had the sinking feeling that Steve couldn't be more right.

Chapter Three

Five hours later, I was pouring Donna Littlefield a glass of Chablis at Eddie's Place, where I had been tending bar on the weekends while our mutual pal, Roxanne, was on bed rest. "What do you know about Naomi Easley?"

Donna, who was the owner of the more popular of the two cut and curl salons in town, arched her perfectly shaped brows. "Other than the fact that she was a shameless gossip, always digging for the latest dirt, not a lot."

I leaned in so that I could hear Donna over the Pat Benatar classic blasting through the speakers mounted over the gleaming oak bar. "What kind of dirt?"

Her sapphire eyes sparkled. "Last time I saw her, all Naomi wanted to talk about was when Ian and I were going to get married."

Ian Dearborn was the hunky veterinarian the two-time divorcée had been dating for the last three months. She had been crazy for Ian when we mooned over him back in high school, and Fozzie adored him, but I wasn't anxious for one of my best friends to follow my mother's lead and rush into another marriage.

Donna's gaze followed two local regulars as they left the bar and disappeared into the adjoining eight-lane bowling alley. Since that was my cue to collect the tip they had left me and clean up behind them, I was about to excuse myself when I noticed her checking the time on her cell phone. "How late is he?"

"Ten minutes. Ian texted me about an emergency surgery that had him running late, but I thought he'd be here by now."

Fine by me that he wasn't, because I needed some alone time with her.

"Hold that thought," I said, dashing to the other end of the bar.

After I had cleared away the dirty glasses and checked in with my other customers, I rejoined Donna. "Back to Naomi Easley. When was the last time you saw her?"

Donna cocked her head, looking at me the way Fozzie does when I ask him what I should make for dinner, only without the wagging tail. "Why are you so interested in Naomi all of a sudden?" She gasped. "Her death *was* an accident, wasn't it?"

"Absolutely." Probably.

I rested my elbows on the bar. "You did her hair fairly regularly, right?"

"Almost every week since I first opened Donatello's."

"Did you ever get the impression that she'd been drinking?"

Donna shook her head and a chunky length of blond hair spilled over her shoulder. "I only ever saw her during the afternoon—a little early for this stuff," she said, taking a sip from her wineglass. "Why?"

"Just curious about something I'd heard."

"Oh, about her being a bit of a wine connoisseur?"

All I knew about was one empty wine bottle, but I was more than willing to tell a little white lie if it kept Donna talking. "Something like that."

"I saw what she jokingly referred to as her wine cellar. Probably no more than five bottles total, but every one of them had a story. All about the vineyard she and her friends visited and the wines they tasted. And then what they had for lunch." Donna dabbed her eyes with her bar napkin. "I'm gonna miss those stories."

I could sympathize with the loss of a favorite story-teller, but the only story I wanted to hear about involved that "wine cellar."

Unfortunately, my bar waitress was signaling me to fill a drink order.

"Duty calls." I looked back at Donna. "Don't move."

But instead of staying put, she slid off the stool and waved at Ian as he stepped around the waitress aiming darts at me from the end of the bar.

Darn it.

"Sorry I'm late," Ian said, planting a kiss on Donna's cheek after he gave me a perfunctory wave.

"It's no big deal. Char kept me company."

Yeah, and I wasn't done with her yet.

"Shall we?" Ian guided Donna to an available table near the back wall while I tried to set a land speed record as a mixologist.

After filling that drink order, I grabbed a couple of laminated menus and made my way to their table.

Ian grinned at me when I handed him a menu. "Well, you certainly get around. Are you our waitress tonight, too?"

"Nope." Libby, the fifty-something waitress Eddie recently hired, had yet to warm up to me, and I didn't need her to think I was trying to ace her out of a tip. "Think of me like one of those substitute teachers we had in high school. I'm just taking drink orders and hoping that no one tries to play stump the newbie. Although I do have Eddie's mixed-drink bible if you want something exotic."

He glanced at the menu. "Whatever pale ale you have on tap works for me."

"I'm good," Donna said, clearly still on her best behavior since she rarely had more than one drink in front of a guy she wanted to impress.

You're trying to be. And apparently succeeding, because Ian could hardly take his eyes off the blond beauty sitting across from him.

"I'll be back in a flash." When I stepped behind Ian, I motioned for Donna to follow me.

"What's up?" she asked, joining me seconds later at the bar as I reached for a glass.

"Nothing. I'm just short-handed, so if you don't mind delivering this to Ian…"

"Oh, is that all. I thought you wanted something."

She knew me too well. "Actually, there is one thing. I was wondering when you had the opportunity to see Naomi Easley's wine cellar."

"Hon, it was hardly a wine cellar. Just a rack on her kitchen counter."

And not at all what I cared about. "*When* were you over at her place?"

Donna cocked her head at me again. "I was going every other Sunday for the last few months. Ever since I started doing Althea Flanders' hair."

The name sounded vaguely familiar, but I didn't get the connection to Naomi. "Wine-tasting buddy?"

"Maybe once upon a time. Between all the little strokes and the fall she took at her husband's funeral, it's been easier for me to go to her. I give her sister Mavis a trim if she wants one, and then go across the street to take care of Naomi. At least, that was my routine until last month."

I set the glass of golden-yellow ale in front of her. "Do you remember which Sunday you last saw her?"

Donna's long lashes fluttered as a tear rolled down her flawless, peachy cheek. "Kind of hard to forget, considering it was the day she died."

Whoa.

I handed her another napkin. "But while you were there she seemed okay?"

"She complained about her knees, but that was normal," Donna said, drying her eyes.

Maybe so, but what happened later sure wasn't. "Thanks. You should probably get back." I looked past her at the annoyed bleached blonde standing at Ian's table. "I think my waitress is ready to take Ian's order."

Donna straightened the pumpkin spice V-neck sweater

hugging her curves. "How do I look?"

"Beautifully seasonal." One of the guys sitting near the taps signaled for a refill, so I shooed her away. "Go have fun."

Donna waved at someone near the door. "You too," she said, smiling back at me as my favorite detective rounded the bar.

Filling a glass, I felt my mood lighten when Steve claimed the seat that Donna had just vacated. "Did you just get here?" I asked.

He pointed at the glass in my hand. "Pour me one of those, and no. I saw that huddle you were in with Donna and thought you might need a minute, so I went to the other side to say hi to Eddie."

More like yell at Eddie, since the bowling alley side of this converted brick warehouse played the same classic rock as the tavern, only it was cranked up a couple decibels to accompany tonight's atomic bowling event for the teens not going to Homecoming.

Steve was glancing back in Donna's direction when I delivered his beer. "So is there trouble in paradise?" he asked.

"Huh?"

"With those two. Or is it girl stuff that I'm not supposed to know?"

Given the fact that Steve considered the subject of Naomi Easley's death to be closed, I was okay with taking the out he had just given me. "It's nothing you want to hear about." And I wasn't about to tell him.

✳

"Earth to Charmaine," my grandmother called out to me a few minutes after we left the church parking lot the next morning.

I glanced over at the woman giving me the *look* from the passenger seat. "Sorry, what?"

"I knew you weren't listening."

"I was just thinking about something else." Because I couldn't understand why a woman who had just had her hair done would want to risk unfurling all those curls by soaking in a bath. "What were you saying?"

"I said if you and Stevie didn't have plans for later, I could pop a roast in the oven for dinner."

While I was certain that Steve would be up for joining my grandmother for a meal, since he'd been called to the scene of a burglary late last night, I couldn't be sure when he'd be up for me to ask. "Sounds good to me. But Steve was up really late and—"

"Are you sure I want to hear this?" Gram asked, making reference to the "Don't ask, don't tell" policy that had governed all discussion of my love life ever since I moved back home to Port Merritt.

"It was police business that had nothing to do with me."

"Oh. You seemed so dreamy-eyed about whatever you were thinking about, I just assumed ... Well, that you'd had a ..." She cleared her throat. "You know, a *satisfying* evening."

Good grief.

I needed to change the subject, pronto. "Actually, I was thinking about Donna."

"Donna!" Gram slumped back in her seat as I rounded the corner where her two-story Victorian sat like a grand dame looking out over her less stately neighbors. "I wouldn't have guessed that in a million years. Not with that faraway look on your face. What's going on with her?"

Nothing that Gram didn't already know, since Donna dating one of the most eligible bachelors in town was well-circulated gossip circuit news. "It's not so much what's going on now as it is what happened on the day that Naomi Easley passed away," I said, pulling into Gram's carport.

When I killed the engine and reached behind me for my tote bag, Gram pressed her hand to my arm. "Not so fast. What do you mean 'what happened'?"

"It's probably nothing."

She scowled. "Doesn't sound like nothing. So start talking."

Since I wanted to give Steve another hour of sleep before heading across the street to ask him about dinner, and possibly get a brunch date out of him, I was in no hurry to leave. Plus, I knew there was a full pot of coffee waiting inside.

"Over coffee," I said.

She flung off her seatbelt. "Now you're talkin'."

Twenty minutes and half a pot later, Gram's scowl had made a comeback. "That seems awfully strange."

"I know! Ever since Donna told me about doing Mrs.

Easley's hair that day, I haven't been able to make sense of her being discovered in that bathtub."

"Of course, it's all anyone wanted to talk about at the funeral, but even then her being found that way struck me as highly unlikely."

"It certainly isn't what I would do if I'd just paid someone to curl my hair."

Gram shook her head. "Sweetie, I'm not talking about her hair. I know for a fact that Naomi was concerned about the big step into her tub. At the last garden club meeting Florence even suggested that she should get a walk-in. Less fall risk and she could get therapy jets for her achy joints."

"You think that she let that big step stop her? I know Mrs. Easley wasn't very tall, but she seemed pretty agile for a woman her age."

Gram aimed her scowl at me. "I happen to be the same age."

I stifled a sigh. "I wasn't trying to imply that everything has to fall apart once you hit eighty. I just meant that she seemed to be perfectly capable of climbing into a bathtub."

"Maybe so, but after falling at her house a couple years back and breaking her collarbone, Naomi made it sound like she wanted to minimize all chances of history repeating itself."

And that safety-minded woman ends up drowning in her bathtub? "Then this really doesn't make sense."

Chapter Four

"Oh, I almost forgot to tell you about the interesting phone call I got a couple of hours ago," my grandmother called out from the living room while Steve and I finished with the dinner dishes.

Steve handed me a plate to dry. "Any idea what she's talking about?"

"Not a clue." But it had better not have anything to do with any of her recently departed friends.

I returned the plate to its home in the cupboard and went in through the dining room to hear about this mystery phone call. "This isn't about ..." I lowered my voice. "Mrs. Easley's death, is it? Because now definitely isn't the time."

Leaning back in her recliner, Gram shook her head. "Honey, nobody's talking about that but you."

Oh.

Gram brightened while she stroked Myron, the fat orange tabby purring on her lap. "I heard from your mom."

So had I when I received a text from Marietta earlier

in the afternoon. "I assume she told you about some interview she did with a *Today* show producer."

"Yes, she expects it to run tomorrow or Tuesday, so we're all supposed to record the show so we don't miss it."

Smiling contentedly, Gram handed me the remote control to her cable box. "If you wouldn't mind."

I didn't, but since she typically didn't need my help recording any of her favorite late-night shows, I felt a private conversation coming on. "Do you need a refresher course on how to set the recorder?"

"Not when I have you to do it for me. And as long as we're discussing this new movie of your mother's, I wanted to ask how you felt about throwing her a little welcome-home celebration next Sunday."

I finished setting the recording for both telecasts and handed back the remote. "Since Barry's flying down Friday to do the red carpet premiere thing with her, they might not want to party as soon as they get home."

"Your mother not wanting to be made a fuss over?" Gram scoffed. "Please."

Okay, she had a point. "But after all the Hollywood hoopla, Barry might want life to get back to normal as soon as possible." Judging by the impression he'd given me yesterday, I was sure of it.

"Then he shouldn't have married an actress."

For Marietta's sake I hoped he wasn't thinking the same thing.

After Gram's front door closed behind us and I gave

Steve the lowdown about her celebration idea, he turned to me with the identical measure of disdain as when I invited him to Rox's baby shower. "A party."

"We all know this movie is a big deal to my mom, so Gram wants us to show our support."

"I might be working that night," he muttered as we crossed the street to his house.

"I haven't told you what night yet."

"You really think that matters?"

Nope, but I wanted the man I loved by my side. "Gram was talking about having a barbecue if the weather's nice."

Steve grunted.

"She was hoping you'd do the flesh-searing honors."

"After basking in a week of public glory, your mother is going to be—"

"Insufferable. I know. She was well on her way before she left to go on her publicity tour, so I completely understand." I followed Steve to his front step and wrapped my arms around his neck. "But I'll make it worth your while to say yes."

"Yeah? What kind of bribe do you have in mind?"

"Hmmm." I pulled him close, soaking in the warmth radiating from his solid chest. "Do this little favor for me, and I'll let you come over and use my new elliptical machine anytime you want."

Steve's dark eyes gleamed with carnal intent. "I already come over anytime I want."

"But now you can get a workout in."

"I can think of another way to get a workout in," he

said, pulling me onto the hardwood of his entryway when he opened the door. "If you're up for getting a little exercise."

"I am if you are." Just as Steve was about to lower his lips to mine, I pressed my palms against his pecs. "Assuming, of course, that you're up for a little celebration with my mother."

Taking my hand, he marched me down the hall to his bedroom.

That would be a *yes*.

The next morning, after dragging my weary butt up the chipped marble steps of the late nineteenth-century courthouse, I had an unexpected sight upon entering the county prosecutor's third-floor office.

Patsy Faraday, the legal assistant typically stationed outside Frankie's office like a gatekeeper, was nowhere to be seen. Her computer monitor wasn't on, nor was there a scrap of paper on her tidy desk. Considering that it was 8:03 and Patsy, the human time clock, wasn't around to give me any grief about my lack of punctuality, this was a nice way to ease into a Monday.

Making it even better, Frankie was waving me into her office.

After an exchange of morning pleasantries, my boss solved the mystery of the empty desk. "Patsy had a miserable weekend because of a toothache, so she's at the dentist's this morning. I assume you have plenty to keep you busy?"

"Yes, ma'am." I had already been enlisted to assist the deputy criminal prosecutor with the narcotics trafficking case coming to trial next month. That would guarantee me many hours of prep busywork, but it didn't mean that I couldn't take on another assignment of particular interest. "Unless there's something that I can do in Patsy's absence. Any pending cases that need some follow-up? Maybe some details that need to be chased down?"

Leaning back in her desk chair, Frankie shook her head, the puckers surrounding her raspberry-painted lips betraying her reluctance to allow me to stick so much as a pinkie into Patsy's territory. "No, I don't believe so."

Dang.

Since I had cracked the door open to the case that kept rattling around in my brain, I figured that I might as well step through with both my size eights. "Speaking of pending cases, one of Naomi Easley's neighbors approached me over the weekend to express his concern about the way she died."

"I imagine this would be the same gentleman who made the nine-one-one call."

I nodded. "Leland Armistead."

Frankie's slate-blue eyes grew wary behind her wireframe bifocals. "And what did you say to Mr. Armistead?"

I knew I had better exercise caution in choosing the next few words to come out of my mouth. "Nothing, really. I was in a hurry at the time, but he made it pretty clear that he had been expecting some sort of follow-up visit as part of an investigation."

Wouldn't that be a good thing for me to do?

"Steve spoke to him at some length when he responded to that call, so I don't think any follow-up by this office is warranted."

Double dang.

I heard a rap behind me and turned to see barrel-chested Deputy Criminal Prosecutor Ben Santiago filling most of the doorway.

Holding a stack of manila files in his arms, he aimed his gaze at the sixty-one year-old behind the oak desk. "Do you need a few more minutes?"

"No, we're done." Frankie gave me a cool smile. "Thank you, Charmaine."

Dang, dang, and dang again. I'd just been dismissed.

"Stop by and see Odette when you have a minute," Ben said to me, referring to his legal secretary. "She has a little copy project for you."

"Okay." It wasn't the assignment I had been hoping for when I stepped into this office, but at least I'd dangled it in front of Frankie to see if she'd bite.

It had been worth a shot, I thought, clicking the door shut behind me.

Then another thought struck me that put a spring in my step when I rounded the bend toward the administrative assistant bullpen. Frankie didn't explicitly tell me *not* to talk to Mr. Armistead.

I just couldn't do it as a representative of her office.

But as Leland Armistead had reminded me, he and I were old friends. So what that I barely remembered him. No one here should bat an eye at me visiting an old friend.

Especially if I just happened to be in the neighbor-hood—something that another old friend might be able to help me with.

Chapter Five

Donna's eyes lit up when the little silver bell over the door of her salon announced my arrival shortly before she closed at six.

"Hey," she said, angling around the long legs of the strawberry blonde in her chair to hit each perfectly coiffed tendril with a mist of hair spray. "You picked the perfect time to stop by, because we're just wrapping up."

Considering that her customer, Renee Ireland, the newshound for the Port Merritt *Gazette*, had an assessing smile on her full lips as she looked up at me, I begged to differ. Because there was no way that I was going to bring up the subject of the visit I wanted to pay to Naomi Easley's neighbors in front of a reporter.

Instead, I eased onto the empty swivel chair next to her and grabbed the length of my ponytail. "You know how you've wanted to whack on this? I think I'm ready for a little change."

Donna patted Renee's arm. "And you said it was a slow news day. There's some breaking news for you."

The fifty-ish reporter dropped the smile. "Right," she

said, sharpening her gaze on me as Donna removed the plastic cape from her shoulders. "But there is some news breaking this week that I think my readers would be interested in—what's going on with your mother, now that she has a movie coming out."

Renee had written a feature several months back about my mom's return to her hometown shortly after filming wrapped up, so I wasn't shocked by the reporter sniffing around for a follow-up. But given the fact that Marietta had agreed to that interview *before* she discovered that Renee had been Barry Ferris's ex-girlfriend, I didn't want to get sucked into the vortex of that old love triangle. "Marietta gets home this weekend, after the premiere, so maybe you'd like to ask her yourself."

"I hear Barry will be walking her down the red carpet," Renee said, flaunting that tidbit of insider knowledge with icy satisfaction.

Since she hadn't heard that from me, and my grandmother would have mentioned it if someone from the local paper had called, that left just the one person to disclose his plans: Barry Ferris. "I wouldn't be surprised if that's what he decided. After all, he is her husband."

Renee flashed a fake smile.

I didn't know which annoyed her most. My refusal to dish any dirt on my mother or the reminder that Barry had married her.

"If you hear from your mom, do let her know that I'd like to talk to her," Renee said, rising to her six-foot height and handing me her business card.

"Will do." Maybe, if the situation presented itself, and

only because we both knew Marietta Moreau craved every opportunity she could get to add some luster to her waning celebrity status.

Donna directed me to take the swivel chair Renee had just vacated, and then while they settled up at the front desk, I looked at my reflection in the mirror. For someone who had spent all of her adult life avoiding identifying with her glamorous mother, why did I have to see her green eyes staring back at me?

Because I was being just as much of an opportunist?

"Maybe this is a bad idea," I said as Donna snapped a black cape behind my neck.

"Don't be ridiculous." Freeing my hair from the elastic band, she shook it loose so that it hung past my shoulder blades like a dirty brown mop head. "Look at this mess. You haven't let me layer it in months."

"Fine. Do your thing, but you should know that the main reason I came is that I need a favor."

She smirked. "Hon, when you show up out of the blue, it's usually because you want something."

I didn't much care for that smirk, but I knew that whatever little bit of irritation she was feeling would soon dissipate. "It's a small something, and it might come off as an odd request, but could I go with you the next time you do Althea Flanders' hair?"

"Why on earth would you want to do that?" Donna asked, guiding me past the front desk to the shampoo bowl.

"I haven't seen her since her husband's funeral. And that's probably the one and only time I met her sister, so

I'm overdue paying them a visit."

"Remember what I just said about you showing up out of the blue?"

"Okay, okay," I said, opting for full disclosure since I had a spray nozzle aimed at my nose. "I want to have a chat with Naomi Easley's neighbors."

"If her death was an accident, why—"

"I'm not saying it wasn't an accident. It's just so weird that they found her in that bathtub, I can't stop thinking about it."

"Tell me about it. I could be the last person to see the poor thing alive."

Closing my eyes while Donna doused my head with warm water, I thought of her doing the same thing to Naomi. "So she didn't mention having any plans for later?"

"Oh, I had forgotten about that. She did say that she'd be looking good for a little date she had that evening. When I asked her if she had a beau, she laughed it off. Said it was just a gin rummy date with a neighbor." Donna sighed. "I guess she never made it."

Obviously not. But why did Naomi chase down a bunch of pills with a bottle of wine if she had plans for later?

After I left the salon with Donna's promise to pick me up Sunday on her way to Althea's condo, I headed home, where Fozzie immediately led me to the detective using my new elliptical machine.

Since he was wearing a Port Merritt PD polo and cotton slacks instead of sweats, Steve clearly hadn't come over for the exercise. "A little overdressed for a workout, don't you think?"

Giving me a sexy grin, he slowed to a stop. "That depends on what you have in mind."

I was hungry and tired and had only one thing in mind. "Dinner out somewhere?"

"Then I'm not so overdressed after all," he said, stepping off the pedals. "Did you notice anything when you came in?"

I fluffed my newly layered bob to clue him in that he also had something to notice. "Other than you look like you came here straight from work, no." I glanced down at the canvas tool bag by his feet that Fozzie was sniffing. "But it does appear that Mr. Fix-it came with you."

Steve gave me a peck on the lips. "To fix that squeak of yours."

He made it sound like a personal problem. "I beg your pardon. I don't have any parts that squeak."

"Not anymore you don't."

Not that I had ever heard it because I had yet to use my newly acquired exercise equipment. But if Steve wanted to rid me of Marietta's excuse of avoidance, my saddlebag thighs were quick to remind me to show some gratitude. "Thanks. I appreciate that."

"How much?"

I held out my arms as wide as they would go. "This much."

"Is that all? My labor doesn't come cheap, you know."

I wrapped my hands around his neck and kissed him until we were both breathless.

"That's better," he said, holding me close. "But I had something else in mind."

"Yeah?" I didn't mind burning a few calories before indulging in the cheesy tacos I hoped to talk him into later.

I reached for the tab of his zipper, but Steve took my hand before I found purchase.

He pressed a kiss to my fingertips. "I was referring to you buying dinner."

Even better. "Deal if I get to pick the place."

"As long as they serve tacos."

He was a man after my own heart. My stomach, too. "If you insist."

When I started for the door, the black fur ball that had been trying to wedge between us raced in front of me. "I'll just feed him first."

"Already done. Fed *and* watered, so let's go." Stepping around the chow mix tapping his toenails in the entryway, Steve's gaze softened as he fingered a lock of my hair. "And yes, I like your haircut."

"You noticed."

"What can I say? As a detective I tend to notice stuff."

"Yessir, it's hard to slip anything by you," I said, my thoughts drifting toward what little I'd been able to glean about his most recent death investigation.

But it wasn't entirely impossible.

Chapter Six

After waking up to a text from my mother confirming that the *Loving Lucian* cast interviews would run in the second hour of the *Today* show, I wasn't a bit surprised when my cell phone started ringing the instant I arrived at the office.

I didn't have to look at the display to know that it was Marietta again. *Sheesh, I got the message. I'm recording the show.*

Now was not the time to deal with an excited mother, not when I could see Patsy giving me the stink-eye from her hall monitor post.

"Welcome back," I said to Patsy after the call went to voice mail. "How are you feeling?"

With a determined set to her pointy chin, the tawny-haired legal assistant with the gray roots glared at the computer monitor in front of her. "I'll live."

The angry swelling of her jaw line gave me fair warning to tread lightly in her vicinity. Unfortunately, the phone in my tote bag chose that moment to start chirping again like a hungry bird.

Patsy slanted her glare in its direction like she wanted to wring its little neck.

I reached into my tote to silence it and then spotted Rox's name as the caller ID. "What's up?" I asked, rushing into the break room so that if she were calling to tell me that she was in labor, I wouldn't scream in Patsy's ear and become the next neck to be wrung. "Is it time?"

"No. I've resigned myself to the fact that this kid doesn't ever want to come out."

Dropping my tote on the table in the center of the room, I pulled out a chair. "Patience is a virtue."

"I'm fresh out. But never mind that. Tell me that you're near a TV 'cause I just turned on the *Today* show and—"

"My mother's on. I know."

"She's on, too?"

"What do you mean, *too*?"

"Chris is on. This very minute, teaching the co-hosts how to make chicken parmesan."

I knew that my ex-husband had recently released a cookbook. No doubt to cash in on his celebrity chef status after rocketing to fame on a cooking channel. "Good for him," I said, trying not to sound as bitter as the coffee dregs simmering at the bottom of the carafe ten feet away.

"Uh-huh. That scored a negative nine on the sincerity meter, but considering he was such a jerk, I think you're being generous."

"How's he doing?" I winced, hating myself for caring.

"You should turn on a TV there and see for yourself.

He's making love to the camera like someone crowned him Prince Charming of the kitchen."

Of course he was.

"Eww, I have to warn you, though. These chicks are fawning over Chris so much that you'll probably spit up in your coffee."

There was a flat screen mounted in the conference room across the hall, but after almost two years of watching my ex's charmed life from a distance, my dumped ass felt no compunction to see it in high defini-tion. "My grandmother's recording it. I can watch later."

"Just as well. They're talking about his cookbook now, so it sounds like they're wrapping up."

That was also what we should do so that Patsy didn't come in and catch me on the phone instead of making coffee.

And then Rox uttered a breathy "Oh, my."

I waited, expecting some sort of blow-by-blow ac-count of what she was watching. "What?"

"Are you freaking kidding me?"

"What?!"

"Your ex just made a little announcement," Rox said, making it sound like I wouldn't be happy to hear it.

"How little?"

"Uh... actually, pretty major."

Chris already had the book out that he'd been hyping, he'd had the TV deal for over a year, and he and his supermodel girlfriend had become social media darlings since getting together over the holidays. How much more fairy dust needed to rain down on the prince who couldn't see his happily-ever-after happening with me?

"Honey," Rox said with an ache in her voice. "He's engaged."

Almost ten hours later, I sat cross-legged on my grandmother's living room floor and stared transfixed at my ex-husband's beaming face as he announced the news of his engagement to golden-haired, Danish beauty Raina Lassen.

"Look at the act he's putting on," Gram muttered from her recliner. "That bozo's never looked that happy in his life."

Certainly not in his life with me.

I paused on the moment when the camera got a tight shot of Chris's jubilant face as he waved to the bride-to-be to join him onstage. "It's no act." And why should it be? Chris now had the "more" he'd admitted he wanted the night he walked out of our marriage.

"I get what the turkey sees in her," Gram said when I played the rest of the segment. "Look at her. She's a stunner. But what does she get out of that relationship beyond a temperamental chef to do all the cooking?"

I backed up to the part when Raina stepped out to join him wearing zebra-striped leggings, no doubt in a size that mere mortals past the age of puberty shouldn't be allowed to fit into. "I don't think she eats much." Beyond that I didn't want to know.

"Maybe not, but I see a little belly."

All I could see was impossibly long, shapely legs.

"Doubtful. She's a swimsuit model."

"Not over the next six months, she's not."

"What?" While I froze the image where the camera zoomed in on Raina, a pair of pink fuzzy slippers appeared at my right.

"Yes, sirree. That girl's gonna be eating for two." My grandmother stabbed an arthritic finger in the direction of the flat screen where Raina was running a graceful hand over an unmistakable baby bump. "'Cause there's a bun in that oven."

I shuddered, the air vacating my lungs as if I'd been sucker-punched by the guy who had insisted that he never wanted to have children.

"You okay, honey?" Gram asked.

"Sure." I was just surprised is all. Because my ex had been a much better liar than I'd given him credit for.

I pressed *play* to demonstrate how okay I was. Which might have been a good plan if Chris hadn't kissed the future Mrs. Scolari's cheek with such crushing tenderness that it made my eye sockets burn.

"He makes nice with the cameras rolling, but a tiger doesn't change his stripes. And that one there showed himself to be a real selfish bastard. For the sake of the little one, though, I hope they make it work."

For the sake of the baby that I had once wanted with that bastard, I sure hoped that my grandmother was right.

After several hours of fielding calls from well-intended friends and family members, including a ticked-off mother whose interview got cut for time, it came as a relief to hunker down the next morning with a copy machine that didn't want to talk about my feelings.

Some of the ladies working on the third floor who had known me most of my life gave me sympathetic smiles when we passed in the hallway, so the news about my ex had obviously made the rounds.

As Donna had reminded me when she called last night, soon this would be yesterday's news and it would all blow over. Marietta's movie would come out and she would once again be the Digby that everyone in Port Merritt wanted to talk about. In the meantime, I just needed to act like Chris's latest media foray was of no consequence to me, which it wasn't.

Not really.

Of course, it would be much easier to talk myself into that little lie if I hadn't just stepped into Duke's for lunch and seen all heads turn to me.

Good grief.

"Is there something going on here that I should know?" I asked my great-uncle as I entered his kitchen.

The tall man flipping a greasy hamburger patty knitted his bushy silver eyebrows. "Not anymore there's not."

I cringed. "Want to fill me in?"

Scowling through the cut-out window over the grill at the approaching grandmotherly waitress giving him a dirty look, Duke vented a breath. "Unlike some people, I know when to keep my mouth shut."

"Hey, I'm not the one who started it," Lucille Kressey

protested, coming to a stop in her squeaky orthopedic shoes to tack an order ticket to the aluminum wheel in front of her longtime boss. She looked around the wheel at me. "And Miriam sure didn't mean any harm."

Huh?

The only Miriam I knew was a Duke's regular and one of Lucille's favorite gossip wranglers. "Why do I need to know that?"

Lucille's light blue eyes widened with alarm. "Uh… Steve didn't tell you?"

My heart sunk to the pit of my churning stomach. "What have you done?"

Chapter Seven

"If I had seen Steve sitting at the counter, I would have nipped all that wedding nonsense in the bud," Lucille said, sitting across from me at my great-aunt Alice's butcher block worktable.

"But you didn't." Despite the heat radiating from the industrial oven at my back, I shivered with dread. "And now Miriam's acting like the town bookie so that your pals can bet on when we're getting married." As if I were obligated to keep up with the brisk race-to-the-altar pace set by my ex and Marietta.

"I didn't place a bet, if that makes you feel any better."

I glared at Lucille. "It doesn't."

Alice patted my hand. "Sorry, hon. You know what sport those old biddies like to make out of all the he-ing and she-ing goin' on in these parts."

"And I know for a fact that Miriam was embarrassed to have Duke tell her to knock it off," Lucille added. "She even went over and apologized to Steve."

I pushed back from the table to make myself a turkey

sandwich to go. Although after I marched the two blocks to the police station to offer my own apology and met the stony gaze of the detective climbing out of his unmarked sedan, my appetite made a run for it. Exactly what my feet wanted to do.

"Have you had lunch?" I asked, holding up the white paper sack in my hand like a peace offering.

Joining me on the cracked sidewalk, Steve glanced at the bag as if it might be worthy of target practice. "That depends."

"On what?"

"On what you brought me."

"Half a turkey sandwich and an apology."

Grimacing as if neither held much appeal, he headed toward the shade-covered wooden bench across the street. "Sounds like we'd better sit down, then."

Taking the seat next to Steve, I pulled out one of the sandwich halves from the paper sack and offered it to him.

He shook his head. "You don't need to give me your lunch. And since I can guess where it came from, there's absolutely nothing that you need to apologize for."

I tossed the sandwich back into the bag on my lap. "Still, I'm sorry," I said, wishing it were that easy to hide the burn of embarrassment flaring in my cheeks. "I guess some of the ladies saw Chris announce that he was getting married."

"Yep, pretty safe guess."

Steve didn't seem to want to say anything else on the subject of my ex, so I took that as his way of informing me that he had heard enough for one day.

I nodded. "Miriam must've decided that betting on Rox's delivery date wasn't enough sport for them."

"She is overdue," Steve added as if that helped explain away some of the insanity from this morning.

"And is very ready to welcome that baby into the world."

Steve wrapped his arm around my shoulder. "I'm sure."

And I was pretty sure he was as relieved to have something else to talk about as I was. "I know Eddie is, too."

"That would be a safe bet."

No, no, no. We were not going to tiptoe back toward the subject of wagering on our wedding date.

I held the paper sack in front of his nose. "Are you sure you're not hungry? It's a yummy sandwich if I do say so myself." And if we ate, we wouldn't have to talk.

"I'm sure it is, but I wouldn't want to spoil my appetite for later."

I relaxed into his warmth. "Are you taking me out later?"

"It's Wednesday."

The evening we had a standing dinner invitation at my grandmother's. "Oh, yeah."

"We're still on like usual, right?"

"You bet." *Crap!* Just when I thought I had averted the impending disaster of Miriam's stupid betting pool, I managed to push us back to the precipice of that debacle's deep end.

"Something wrong?" he asked when I sat up straight with my cheeks on fire.

"No, why?"

"You're blushing."

Gathering my bags, I got to my feet. "Don't be ridiculous. I just realized that I need to get back to work. That's all."

"Of course. A perfectly natural reaction."

I didn't believe him for a second, but if he was willing to play along, so was I. "Absolutely."

"A safe wager, one might say."

In no mood to acknowledge the evil gleam in his eyes, I turned on my heel. "I think we're done here."

Because there was nothing safe about it. Not to my head and definitely not to my heart.

Steve's pickup wasn't in his driveway, so I assumed I was the first to arrive when I greeted my grandmother around six that evening.

"What's for dinner?" I asked, looking through the window of her oven at a casserole dish bubbling with cheese. "It smells awesome."

"Chicken parmesan." Gram looked up from the radish she was slicing into a salad. "After an evening of watching that jerk make it with all that cheese, I came away with a powerful hankering for it."

The only hankering I came away with was to throw all that gooey cheese in my lying ex's face.

"I used low-fat mozzarella like I usually do, though."

Gram's lips curled conspiratorially. "Let all that fat go to his love handles instead of ours."

I stole a cherry tomato from the salad bowl in front of her. "You're my kind of girl. Anything I can do?"

Typically, the answer to that question was to make myself comfortable, so it got my attention when she hesitated.

"I hate to ask, and this isn't anything that needs to be done tonight…" Gram used her paring knife to point at the white banker box on her kitchen table. "But Florence obviously didn't look inside all those boxes she had us pick up last Saturday, because that one there was mislabeled."

I lifted the lid and peeked inside at what appeared to be the contents of some desk drawers that someone had emptied into the box. "So it's not garden club stuff you need to hold onto?"

"No, mercifully. But in case there's anything important in there, it should go back to Naomi's family fairly soon, so if you wouldn't mind. Her daughter's still living in Naomi's house south of the park, so it's practically on your way home."

"No problem," I said, securing the lid. In fact, this provided me with a good excuse to have a little chat with a family member without anyone around here raising so much as an eyebrow.

"I'll take it to my car now so I don't forget about it later." And to get it out of view of the inquisitive cop who would be arriving any minute.

No sooner than those words came out of my mouth

the front doorbell rang.

"That'll be Stevie." Gram looked expectantly at me.

Dang. The owner of the eyebrow I was most worried about raising.

Still, it wasn't like I had anything to hide. Gram hadn't asked me to do anything unethical. Quite the contrary. I just didn't want her to volunteer any details about our conversation to the great-looking guy on her doorstep, or mention my ex. Steve and I simply needed to have a nice, normal meal together, and given how we were about to chow down on my ex-husband's favorite chicken recipe, fat chance of that happening.

"Hope I haven't kept you girls waiting," Steve said.

"Nope. Your timing is impeccable." More than you know. "Dinner's almost ready."

Steve dropped a quick kiss on my lips as he came in holding a white envelope. "Good, I'm starved."

I pointed at his hand. "What do you have there?"

"Your granny's mail. It came to me by mistake."

"What is it?" Gram asked from behind the stove.

"Looks like junk mail." Steve crossed the room to the kitchen table and set the envelope next to the box. "What's with the box?"

Gram gave it a dismissive wave. "Probably more junk, but someone else can make that determination."

Steve turned to me for a translation. "Huh?"

I wanted the first someone to make that determination to be me and scooped up the banker box before he asked any more questions about it. "It's just stuff that she's getting rid of."

"Yeah? Looks heavy, so allow me," he said, taking it out of my clutches.

Crap.

Steve headed for the back door that I was holding open for him. "Want this in the trunk or backseat?"

"Backseat." What I didn't want was more questions about it and followed him to my car to avoid eliciting commentary from the kitchen.

"Garden club junk, huh?"

"What?"

Waiting for me to open the car door for him, Steve dropped his gaze to the orange lettering on the box lid.

"Yeah. It's odds and ends that Gram has no use for." Sort of true.

"What're you going to do with it?"

Since it came from the site of a possible murder, "I'll see if there's anything in there that I can use."

After he loaded the box into my backseat, Steve gave me an easy grin. "Play your cards right and I'll come over later to help you."

No, no, no. This was not something I wanted his help with. "Or we could find something else to do."

He closed the distance between us. "Even better."

I melted into Steve's arms, relaxing for the first time today. *Much better.*

Chapter Eight

After Steve kissed me good night at the door, I waited until I saw him pull out of my driveway before I started digging through the contents of the box that had been screaming for my attention the last four hours.

With the black fur ball at my feet as the least judgmental witness to my snooping that I could ask for, I still felt as if I were invading Naomi's privacy by rifling through her belongings. But she wasn't here to protest, and someone needed to make some effort to investigate the "murder" that her neighbor had reported, right?

Steve would be quick to answer that the someone in question shouldn't be me, but he wasn't here either. So I snapped on a pair of the latex gloves I carried for the occasional death scene investigation and pulled the lid off the box.

Ten minutes later, I had sorted the contents into three piles, covering most of my dining room table top.

The sizable collection of ballpoint pens embossed with the name and address of local merchants indicated only one thing to me: Naomi liked her freebies. I remembered my grandmother once telling me that Naomi's late husband had been a vice president at Chimacam Bank, so I wasn't surprised to see the bank's logo on the better pens. Same deal with the ones with the ergonomic grips from Durand and Terry Realty. Obviously, companies serious about wooing clients with money were willing to spend a little more to entice them to sign on the dotted line.

Mixed in with the pens were some pencils, assorted rubber bands and paper clips, a box of staples, a ruler, some felt markers, an eraser, and a book of postage stamps. It was the typical array of stuff I'd expect to find in a desk, so it looked all the more that someone had emptied a drawer or two into the banker box.

My second pile contributed to the weight of the box but as Leland Armistead had suggested, there was nothing the least bit elucidating about two reams of paper and a few gently used ruled tablets.

That left six file folders, each thick with paper and each with a handwritten label: Phone, Utilities, Bank, Insurance, Medical, and House.

Leafing through the Phone and Utilities folders, it became immediately apparent that Naomi was a stickler for organization, with every account statement filed by date. This also held true for the Bank, Insurance, and Medical folders. But they had something else in common: Not one of them contained a statement for the last three years. Maybe that was why it all got dumped into a mislabeled box and left behind. There were no family keepsakes, no cards or letters to evoke loving memories. It was just a lot of paper that I guessed no one particularly cared about.

I wasn't so sure that should be the case, though, when I opened the House folder and discovered a comparative market analysis done almost two years ago by Durand and Terry. A signed sales agreement followed along with several pages of handwritten notes. Clearly, Naomi had once intended to sell her home. Yes, this still came under the heading of old news and might accomplish little more than to explain how she came by some of the nicer pens. But if Naomi's family had plans to sell her house as part of settling her estate, they might find this information helpful.

"All the more reason for me to go over there tomorrow," I said to Fozzie, who was stirring at the base of my chair while I helped myself to a couple of pens. "What do you think, blue or black?"

Fozzie responded by resting his head on my thigh as if I should spend this moment petting him instead of helping myself to someone else's office supplies.

I tossed the pens back into the box and then ran my hand over his ear. "It's not like anyone's going to notice a couple of freebie pens going missing."

That ear twitched as if it couldn't believe the rationalization it had just heard.

"Don't give me that. You know it's true."

Fozzie shot me a sidelong glance.

If I hadn't been looking down at a dog, I would have sworn that he rolled his eyes.

"Stop with the judgment. That's reserved for humans." Especially latently maternal types who would be returning home on Saturday. "Do you know what's for dogs? Cookies!"

Fozzie raced to the kitchen, his toenails tapping in a happy dance in front of the pantry where I kept his bag of biscuits.

"Welcome off that moral high horse, because you, my dear doggy, can be bought."

Two hours later, I was lying in bed with a snoring dog watching my ex-husband's fiancée gush on an entertainment show about her five-carat diamond ring when my phone rang.

No one I knew would call me after midnight, with the exception of my mother, who tended to do her best griping about her latest reviews at this hour. Also an overdue pregnant lady with breaking news.

At the welcome sight of Rox's name, I muted the TV and tossed back the cover, propelling Fozzie to the floor. "Is it time?"

"No," Rox said with a sigh of irritation that rivaled my dog's. "Sorry if I woke you for a false alarm."

I dropped back onto my stack of pillows. "You didn't. I was just watching TV."

"Me, too. In between trips to the bathroom now that this kid is playing footsie with my bladder. How're you doing?"

I was in no mood to provide an honest answer to that question. "Me? I'm fine and dandy."

"Sure you are. Not to pile onto everything that's been going on the last couple of days, but Raina Lassen is talking about her engagement on channel thirteen."

"Good grief," I said, changing the channel. "What show *hasn't* she appeared on this week?"

"It's not just the ring she's showing off, she's making the rounds with other news."

"The baby."

Rox sharply inhaled. "I thought that was just a celebrity gossip magazine rumor."

I pointed at my flat screen as if Rox could see me. "Look at her. There's a reason she's wearing that linen tunic. It's hiding a bump." As opposed to the tunics I wore to hide my butt.

"Hunh. Maybe. Since they're focusing in on that rock on her finger it's hard to tell."

"Keep watching for a wide shot. That hand is going to rest on her belly any minute now. And not just because of the weight of that gaudy rock."

"Don't be bitter. It's a beautiful ring and you know it."

Didn't mean that I had to like it. "Whatever."

Rox didn't respond for several seconds except to yawn.

"There," I said, pointing again when Raina's hand swept over a nonexistent wrinkle at her waistline while the host drooled over the calendar she was promoting. "That's a definite baby bump."

"Oh, I see what you mean. Yep, she's preggers, all right. All glowy and everything, which I find totally depressing, considering how all I did in my first trimester was puke."

She was depressed? As the first Mrs. Christopher Scolari, it was all I could do to not cry at the sight of this super-human.

"It's unfair is what it is," Rox added.

I couldn't argue with her on that point. My sense of justice had felt under assault since the moment I caught Chris cheating on me with his sous-chef. "No kidding."

"How come when I wear linen I get so wrinkled it looks like I slept in it, and she looks as smooth as silk?"

"Some people live charmed lives." And on that point Raina and Chris were perfect for one another, no matter how much it pained me to admit it. "Wrinkles aren't allowed."

"She's what, twenty-two? Twenty-three?"

"Something like that."

"Her time is coming, and speaking as the owner of a hundred new stretch marks thanks to the small human I've been incubating, possibly sooner than she realizes."

I couldn't help but smile. "You're a good friend, but you don't have to say that for my benefit. I'm okay."

"Sure you are. I know you and what you went through with that man. This can't be easy."

"Doesn't matter." I wrapped my arm around Fozzie, who had jumped back up to curl next to me. "All that is ancient history."

"Chris leaving you high and dry a couple of years ago is ancient history?"

"Twenty-two months." But who was counting?

"A whole twenty-two months. Definitely plenty of

time for you to get over it, and all this happy news about your replacement should roll off you like water off a duck's back."

My eyes blurred with tears as I held Fozzie close. "You betcha."

"What does Steve say about all this?"

"Not much."

"You haven't talked to him about it, have you?"

What was I supposed to say to my other best friend who had made it very clear over the years that we wouldn't be having any heart-to-heart discussions about our feelings?

I wiped my eyes. "It hasn't exactly come up in conversation."

"Char, you need to talk to him."

"I will." Maybe.

"Really talk to him, as in have an honest conversation about how you feel about all this."

"Uh-huh."

"In the meantime, you know you can talk to me. Day or night, because until Junior decides to make his grand debut, I won't be sleeping."

"Thanks. I appreciate that, but don't worry about me. I really am okay. It's just been a crappy little week."

"But it's only Wednesday. There's still plenty of time for this week to improve," Rox said at the same time that Fozzie released a noxious dog fart.

"That could happen." But it clearly wasn't going to start happening tonight.

Chapter Nine

I spent the majority of the next morning on a bumpy single-lane county road so that I could deliver a subpoena to a stinky rural route address nineteen miles west of Clatska. The chicken farmer who would be called as a witness to a felony robbery case involving his son wasn't any happier to see me than I had been to park downwind of his coops.

The stench and the guy's surly attitude did the headache I'd woken up with no favors. But once I could breathe easier in the sanctity of my ex's old Jaguar XJ6, I could almost forgive Chris for not replacing the shock absorbers before he begrudgingly handed over the keys to fast-track me out of his life.

"Almost," I grumbled, my teeth rattling when I joined the short procession of slow-moving vehicles following a yellow hulk of a tractor bouncing toward the turnout marked ahead.

That turnout couldn't come soon enough. Because we were almost out of coffee at the office, and I needed to pick up some speed and arrive with reinforcements or I could expect an even bigger headache in the form of a bunch of caffeine-deprived attorneys who could make that chicken farmer's attitude look like chicken feed.

The guy in the four-by-four pickup two vehicles in front of me must have also been in a hurry, because he hit the gas when he swerved wide around the tractor, kicking up dust as it slowed next to a baling wire fence.

Same with the white SUV that followed the four-by-four's lead, giving the tractor a wide berth.

I and the blue full-sized pickup that had been riding my bumper ever since the tractor first came into view followed suit. Only I didn't have the clearance of the SUV and after seeing its left rear tire bounce in and out of a crater in the road, I straightened to avoid it and my right front tire dropped into its twin with a violent thunk that jerked me into the steering wheel.

"You're okay, we're okay," I muttered like a prayer while my body shuddered with the reality that we were far from okay. Because if I had thought the Jag had been a bumpy ride before I slammed into that pothole, the shimmy shake it was now doing kept me in a white-knuckled grip for the remaining twenty-seven-mile drive back to town.

I didn't want to risk doing any more damage than I'd already done, so I headed straight for Bassett Motor Works, my shaky car's home away from home. There I called to ask my grandmother to pick me up while my mechanic buddy, George Bassett Jr., circled the Jag.

"Well?" I asked after I disconnected, stepping into Georgie's shadow as he stared down at what was starting to look to me like a flat tire. "What's the damage?"

He grimaced. "You're not gonna like this."

I already didn't like it. "Just tell me."

The six-foot-six redhead pointed at the fancy rim my ex had paid top dollar for back when we were in culinary school—the *bent* fancy rim. "I know you don't know much about cars, but this is supposed to be round."

I gave him a dirty look. "That much I do know. Is that why the Jag's vibrating like one of those coin-operated massage chairs at the airport? It wants to pull to the left now, too."

"It's not helping, but that sounds like she needs an alignment. New tires, too. These are pretty much bald."

I heaved a sigh, since I had been hoping for another paycheck before I had to spring for a set of new tires. "How much is all this gonna cost?"

Georgie shrugged a meaty shoulder. "Depends."

"On what else you find?" Because he always managed to find something else wrong with the aging minx I'd been driving.

"That too, but mainly it depends on the replacement cost of the rim. High-end ones like you got tend to be pricey."

Given the recent example of my ex's showy five-carat taste, I could almost hear the cha-ching of a cash register. "Of course they do."

"But all total, with your family and friends discount, I don't think this'll run you more than a thousand bucks."

A thousand-dollar pothole? This week just kept getting better and better.

✳

"What happened?" Gram asked, rolling down her window after she parked her SUV next to my car.

"I had a little run-in with a pothole out in farm country. The pothole won."

She frowned at my almost flat tire. "Maybe this should serve as a lesson. That highfalutin vehicle doesn't belong out in farm country."

Maybe not, but until I could afford something more reliable for delivering subpoenas to chicken farmers, it was my only option. "Well, it won't be going anywhere for a few days, so would it be a terrible imposition if I borrowed your car?"

"Not at all. I don't have any plans until mahjong tomorrow, and I can get Sylvia to pick me up."

"Great. I'll get what I need out of my car."

While Gram climbed out of her SUV, I retrieved the white banker box from my backseat so that I could complete my delivery mission later today.

Gram clucked her tongue. "I thought you were going to drop that off on your way home last night."

"It got late and—"

"It got late because you took it home to snoop through all those files, didn't you?"

"Uh…"

"I thought I raised you better than that," she said, popping open the rear hatch.

Avoiding the disappointment in her eyes, I slid the box into the rear cargo area. "I just wanted to see—"

"I don't care." She banged the hatch door shut as if to drive her point home. "It's bad enough that I went through all that stuff. The violation of Naomi's personal information didn't need to be compounded."

"I doubt that she'd consider it much of a violation if the contents of that box could shed some light on the weird way she died," I said to Gram's back as she marched to the passenger side door.

She shot me a glance after I slid onto the driver's seat. "No one in your office thinks that was anything beyond an unfortunate incident, do they?"

No one but me, and I had yet to be entirely convinced. "Nope."

Gram hugged her amber cardigan sweater tight to her chest as if the two minutes away from the heater that she had cranked to eighty had chilled her to the bone.

Blankly staring past the chain link fence, she vented a breath like a pressure cooker releasing some steam. "So, did it?"

"What?"

"Did anything in that box shed any light? Because the only thing of interest I found was the fact that Naomi had planned to sell her house."

I figured the dwindling balance I had noticed on a few of those bank statements might have prompted the decision to sell. "Same," I said, taking a left out of the auto repair parking lot to take Gram home. "She never mentioned listing the house to you or the other ladies?"

Gram shook her head. "Never. And I'm pretty sure someone would have asked her about it if a for-sale sign had ever been posted."

"I wonder what changed her mind." Because unless her financial situation had changed in the last couple of years, Naomi Easley's funeral could have consumed the last of her savings.

"I think I may know," Gram said when I turned right on 5th Street.

"What was it?"

"Not a what, a who."

"Okay, then who?"

"I'll introduce you when we get there."

"Now?" I was already late getting back to the office. "I thought I was taking you home."

"Do you want to find out the answer or not?"

What difference did a few more minutes make on the Patsy wrath-o-meter? "Where to?"

Gram waved me on past the turn for her house. "Keep going up the hill toward the park. We're returning that box."

Five minutes later, I was huffing and puffing, schlepping that banker box up to the creaky wooden porch of an oversized Victorian dollhouse in need of a fresh coat of paint.

"This doesn't pertain to us so I rang the bell," Gram said, pointing to the handwritten NO SOLICITING sign affixed to the brass doorbell fixture with duct tape.

While we waited I rested the box on my hip and looked around. "Are you sure someone's living here?"

Because by the height of the weeds in the overgrown patches of yellowing grass, the front lawn hadn't been mowed in months.

"She's here." Gram edged closer to the door painted in the same shade of royal blue as the trim around the windows. "I can hear a TV. Maybe it's drowning out the doorbell." She rang again, and then rapped several times with an oxidized door knocker that could double as a horseshoe.

An annoyed-looking round face appeared at the leaded glass window to the left of the door.

Gram gave her a friendly wave, and a second later the door opened a few inches.

"Hello," the woman in her mid-fifties said, her dark, wary gaze ricocheting between my grandmother and me as she shielded her body with the heavy door.

"Hi, Robin." Gram motioned for me to come closer. "I don't know if you've met my granddaughter, Charmaine."

Robin nodded, shifting her focus to the box at my hip. "Are you selling something? Because I really don't—"

"Goodness, no," Gram said with a gentle lilt in her tone as if she were speaking with a child. "We're returning some items of your mother's that got mixed in with the garden club stuff that came home with me the other day."

"Oh." The door opened a little wider, revealing a doughy, pear-shaped woman wearing mismatched baggy sweats who still wouldn't look either of us in the eye.

I had expected that she would have swung the door open so that I could carry the box in to the nearest table, but instead the only move Naomi Easley's daughter made was to narrow her eyes. "Like what?"

Since Gram's gentle approach wasn't getting us anywhere, and my flabby biceps were screaming for relief, I set the box down and removed the lid. "You can see for yourself. There are some office supplies, a bunch of old records that you might want for tax purposes—"

"My brother does her taxes. It should go to him."

"Oh, but it's not all tax stuff," Gram said. "Dear, I don't know what your plans are for keeping the house, but you might want to—"

"*I* am keeping the house." Robin clutched the door as though we had come to steal it from her. "That was prearranged."

Prearranged? That wasn't the word I'd use to describe what was left to me in my mother's will.

"Okay, but someday if you decide that it's too much for you, and you're ready to downsize..." Gram pointed at the box. "There's some information in there that you might find very helpful."

"I don't want any of that. Now, if you'll excuse me, I have something on the stove," Robin muttered, shrinking back into the house like a mole craving the safety of its hidey-hole.

My grandmother and I exchanged glances as the blue door unceremoniously clicked shut in our faces.

"Well, I sure am glad that we rushed over here with this box." That was giving me my upper-body workout for the day.

"Hmpf. I guess I shouldn't be too surprised at how

she acted."

Hoisting the banker box back to my side, I followed Gram down the steps from the porch. "I assume that has something to do with your 'who' comment on the way over here."

She nodded but didn't elaborate until we got into the car. "Naomi never went into any detail about her daughter's *problem* other than to suggest that it was a good solution for her to remain in the house for a while." Gram turned to me. "That's pretty much the line she used at a garden club meeting shortly after moving into her condo."

That would have been a couple of years ago, around the same time that Naomi entered into a sales agreement with a real estate agent. So the lady either changed her mind about selling the house, or as my grandmother had suggested, Robin changed her mother's mind for her.

Gram collapsed back into the passenger seat. "I guess I'm going to have to call Gordon to see if he'll pick up his mother's stuff."

"That's the brother who did her taxes?"

"Lives up north somewhere, but he comes to town periodically to help with things. Or at least he used to, when Naomi was still with us."

"I'll give him a call," I said, starting the ignition. "Maybe I could meet him somewhere." Where no one in an official capacity would see me speaking with Naomi Easley's son in a most unofficial capacity.

Chapter Ten

"Took you long enough," Patsy grumbled when I stopped at her desk to hand in my subpoena delivery paperwork.

"I had some car trouble." I figured the less said about it and any subsequent side trips the better, and held up the Red Apple Market sack in my hands. "But I picked up the coffee we needed." Along with the tuna sandwich that I had eaten in the car on the way here.

Patsy aimed her pointy chin at me, condescension dripping from her thinning lips. "Then perhaps you'd like to go make some."

And not stick around for her to saddle me with some sort of crappy assignment as my penance for today's misadventures? Gladly.

I slipped the receipt and change for the coffee on her desk, and made my escape to the break room before she changed her mind.

Ten minutes later, I discovered that Patsy had arranged for me to serve a stint in the copy room penalty box. By the height of the files under the note that she'd left on my desk, my confinement would be a lengthy one.

Oh joy. But I didn't intend to serve my sentence before I spoke to Gordon Easley.

Unfortunately, I didn't have access to his mother's file with his contact information. That left me no other option but to crawl through some less than reliable listings that I found on the internet, but since several of them included Naomi's name as well as Robin's, I called the phone number they had in common.

The business-like woman who answered told me that she could take a message for Gordon.

"Okay, but let me just verify that Gordon is the son of the late Naomi Easley," I said to avoid wasting time leaving a message for the wrong guy.

"What's this about?"

I couldn't blame the woman for the suspicious tone that had lowered her voice almost a full octave.

"It's a long story, but my name is Charmaine Digby, and I'm in possession of some of Mrs. Easley's things that I'd like to return to a member of her family."

"Where are you?"

"Port Merritt."

"Gordon's sister lives there. You should return them to her."

"I tried. She wouldn't take them."

The woman breathed out a heavy sigh. "I swear. Why she can't do the simplest things to help out is beyond me."

Clearly there was quite a bit of water under this family bridge.

"I'm Gordon's wife. We were planning on going over

to Port Townsend this Saturday, so—"

"What a small world. So am I." At least I would be if we could hook up. "I'd be happy to meet you somewhere."

"We were going to do a little antiquing and then catch a matinee."

After she provided the movie time and place, we agreed to meet in the parking lot a half hour before the coming attractions would start to roll.

"That should give us plenty of time to go in and find a good seat. Actually," she added, "I don't think it's going to be very crowded. The reviews haven't been that great, but I still want to see it."

That gave me a bad feeling about one particular movie that would be coming out tomorrow. "Which one is that?"

"*Loving Lucian.*"

I was afraid she was going to say that.

"I'm sort of dragging my husband to it to give him a couple hours of R and R. I'll probably never hear the end of it if the movie's as bad as the two-star review I read made it out to be."

"Hopefully, it was just that one bad review." For all our sakes.

"Are you sure she read the right review?" Gram asked around noon the next day while slicing a tomato for the salad we'd be sharing. "Your mother told me that it was the best script she'd ever read."

Compared to the slasher films Marietta's movie career had been relegated to ever since she hit the big four-oh, that was probably very true.

Sitting at the kitchen table, I paged through a movie review website on my smartphone and read several variations of the same opinion: "I didn't love *Loving Lucian*" and "Melodramatic mess that wasted the talent of its cast."

At least none of the reviews I was speed-reading pointed any of the movie's shortcomings at Marietta. "I don't know which review Gordon's wife read, but the general consensus amongst all the critics on the website I'm looking at is that, at best, it rates three stars out of five."

Gram joined me at the table with two salad bowls. "That's not bad."

It wasn't particularly good either, especially for an aging actress desperate to shine up her fading star. "I'm not seeing Mom's name mentioned anywhere."

Gram shook her head. "Oh, she'll be devastated by that."

"Definitely." Because despite the week-long publicity tour that Marietta had been so thrilled to be a part of, it seemed that the media viewed it as a waste of time to focus on any cast members beyond the headliners.

"Hopefully she's too busy to pay attention to the reviews."

Sure. The likelihood of that happening was the same as me sitting Steve down for that heart-to-heart. Not gonna happen.

My grandmother gave me a look that told me she didn't believe it either. "At least we can give her some kudos on Sunday. Pop some bubbly and all that."

We could do that, but I didn't particularly want this wingding she'd planned to turn into an ego-stroking party for Marietta. "Mom loves any excuse to crack open a bottle of champagne—"

"So when's the movie tomorrow?"

I looked up from the tomato wedge I was about to pop into my mouth. "I wasn't planning on going in to see it. I'm just meeting the Easleys there so I can hand over that box." And see if I could get a read on how they felt about the weird way that Naomi died.

"Of course we're going in."

I almost dropped my fork. "*We* are?"

"You want to support your mother, don't you?" Gram asked, a victorious glint in her hazel eyes.

That was a hardball question if ever I'd heard one. "How am I supposed to answer that?"

She waggled her fork at me. "There's only one right answer, my dear."

"You don't fight fair."

"I'm an old broad. I don't have to. So when did you say you'd be picking me up?"

I heaved a sigh. "Two."

Smiling, Gram forked another bite of salad. "Wonderful. It's a date. Maybe we can even get Stevie to come with us."

And have Steve find out that I lied to him about whose stuff was in that dang box? Not a chance.

✳

"Remember," I said to my grandmother as we pulled into the theater parking lot. "Let me do the talking."

She patted my thigh. "I heard you the first two times, so relax. I only plan to say hello."

I parked in one of the few remaining parking spaces available behind the whitewashed brick building that housed the historic theater and checked for occupants in the nearby cars. "We're a couple minutes early. They might not be here yet."

"Actually, I think that's Naomi's car that just pulled in." Easing out of the passenger seat, Gram stood and waved at the cinnamon-red sedan, guiding them to the open spot next to us like a lot attendant.

Shrugging on a hoodie while I opened the hatch of Gram's SUV, a brisk breeze made me regret that I hadn't brought a heavier coat.

The middle-aged woman clutching the fawn faux leather jacket to her ample bosom as she stepped out of the sedan appeared to have reached the same conclusion.

With Gram exchanging greetings with Gordon at the driver's side door, I knew I wouldn't have much time to glean a little information before everyone would want to get into the theater and out of this wind.

Gordon's wife had a smile fixed to her thin lips that failed to disguise the caution flag waving under the cover of her tortoise-shell glasses. "Charmaine?"

"Thanks for making the time," I said, extending my

hand.

She shook it with a delicate touch almost as frigid as the wind whipping my hair into my face. "No problem. Gordon's probably more interested in what he left behind at the condo than he is in the movie."

She turned to face the heavyset, gray-haired man in his mid-sixties lumbering toward us with my grandmother by his side. "He's not the Marietta Moreau fan that I am. Are you, honey?"

His fleshy, ruddy cheeks darkened. "Now, don't be putting words into my mouth, especially not in front of Eleanor here."

Gram touched the sleeve of the green plaid flannel shirt outlining a belly to rival Rox's. "Don't worry about sparing my feelings. I've suffered through more than my fair share of my daughter's movies." She extended her hand to Gordon's wife. "Nice to see you under happier circumstances, Paula."

The caution flag dropped, replaced by wide-eyed confusion when Paula exchanged glances with her husband. "Yes, what a nice surprise."

Shock to realize that Marietta's mother was the nice old lady playing parking attendant came a lot closer to the truth, but that wasn't the truth I cared to pursue over the next few minutes.

Gram tightened her coat around her. "Gordon, have you met my granddaughter, Charmaine?"

"I don't think so." He gave me a firm handshake. "Probably why I didn't make the family connection when my wife told me you called."

"My condolences on the loss of your mother," I said to move the conversation the direction I wanted it to go.

He squeezed out a jowly grimace of a polite smile. "Thanks."

"I imagine you two have been quite busy since the service," Gram said. "There's always such a long list of things to do after the loss of a loved one."

"There certainly is." Paula pushed back the mass of silver-streaked soft curls that the wind kept blowing across her lenses. "Gordon's been running himself ragged the last few weeks, tending to every last detail."

A rumble deep in his throat accompanied the cool glance that cut to his wife.

She clamped her mouth shut.

The message had been received loud and clear, probably by all of us. *Stop talking.*

Fine with me because I wanted him to start.

"Have there been any nibbles on the house?" I asked to see what he'd be willing to bite on.

Gordon blinked, a trough digging its way between his heavy brows as if I had struck a nerve. "The house?"

"My grandmother mentioned that your mom's house had been listed," I said, giving Gram a nod of encouragement to play along.

After a nanosecond that promised some payback for putting her on the spot, Gram smiled as demurely as an ingénue. "I couldn't help but notice the listing when I looked through the files to prepare for the next garden club meeting."

She pointed at the box with the big orange lettering

behind me, and Paula perked up like Fozzie when I reach into the cupboard for his dog food.

"What listing?" she asked, angling past me to lift the box lid.

Gram peered over Paula's shoulder. "You'll find that everything's in there, just the way I found it. And of course, once I realized the box had been mislabeled, I asked Charmaine to help me return it."

Meeting Gram's gaze, I gave her a little thumbs-up for leaving out the part where I rifled through that box with a lot more interest than Gordon was demonstrating in it.

Which would make complete sense if he had been the one who had packed it.

"Oh, this *old* listing." Paula held up the sales agreement for her husband to see. "I'd almost forgotten that your mom had the house on the market."

Almost? Hardly. By the brittle smile clinging to her tangerine lips, she seemed to be willing Gordon to back her up.

"Yeah." He huffed a weary breath, giving her a knowing look. "That didn't last long."

"It's a woman's prerogative to change her mind," Gram said as if the old cliché could explain the odd exchange we were witnessing. "But I'm quite sure that I saw the for-sale sign on your mom's condo. That was just last weekend. But with the high demand for homes at that complex, maybe it's sold already."

Gordon shook his head. "Not yet."

"The real estate agent we're working with thinks that it might be a little while." Paula tossed the paperwork back into the box. "I guess that's fairly common when someone passes on the premises."

"But it's not like it was a murder," I said, watching Gordon for an emotional reaction.

He winced as if I'd landed a physical blow. "Doesn't matter. No one who knew my mother is going to want to live there."

Which would account for the majority of the seniors in town.

"Give it some time," Gram chimed in. "Maybe after the holidays, prospective buyers will have a fresh perspective on the situation."

Paula nodded, locking eyes with her husband. "That's what I've been saying."

"Uh-huh." Gordon reached into the cargo hold and picked up the box. "Or I do what I should have done months ago, when she first brought it up."

Gram turned to Paula. "Is this about that walk-in tub Naomi wanted a while back?"

Paula blew out a sigh. "We've gone around and around about it. Replacing that bathtub won't change anything. You need to let that go," she said, watching Gordon. "Because what happened isn't your fault."

"Oh yeah?" Gordon slammed his trunk shut and started walking toward the ticket office. "Tell my dead mother that."

Chapter Eleven

"I didn't think that was so bad," Gram said to me as we filed out of the theater. "But I have to admit the movie didn't really hold my attention after Lucian smothered your mother with that pillow."

Given Marietta's reputation for being one of the best screamers in the business, it couldn't have been the first time someone wanted to put a pillow over her mouth.

"Yep, it got slow after that, but Mom's death scene was pretty good."

"*Really* good. And even though I've seen her die at some crazed killer's hands a dozen times, it was tough to watch her struggling to breathe."

"I know." I had to look away more than once. Of course, I was also keeping an eye on Gordon and his wife, who left shortly after my mother's final closeup.

Did that mother-son death scene also hit them a little too close to home?

My gut answered with a resounding *yes*, but despite what Gordon had said, that didn't mean Naomi's death was his fault. I'd spent enough time with grieving loved ones to recognize the self-recrimination that can plague them after a sudden loss. The guilt, the anger, the what-ifs—I'd seen it all before.

Did it convince me to give Gordon Easley a pass after hearing him claim the responsibility for his mother's drowning? Oh, heck no!

"Let me get this straight," Steve said while I poured him a beer during my shift at Eddie's almost two hours later. "You're telling me that the woman drowned because her son didn't give her the kind of bathtub she wanted?"

I leaned across the glossy oak bar separating us so that he could hear me over the crowd watching the Yankees slug their way to the next round in the playoffs. "I'm just telling you what Gordon said to Gram and me."

"That he confessed to negligent homicide by procrastination because the poor guy wasn't crazy about the idea of remodeling her bathroom."

"Sure, make it sound ridiculous." Even more crazy than it sounded when I gave Steve the highlights of that parking lot exchange.

After a glance at the flat screen behind him, he reached for his glass. "Chow Mein, I don't have to try very hard to do that because you seem to be forgetting something."

I didn't mind the use of the nickname Steve gave me back in the third grade, but I couldn't say the same for the smug look that accompanied it.

"After all the self-medicating it appears that Naomi Easley did that night... it wouldn't have mattered if that tub had been easy enough for a two-year-old to crawl out of. She was probably so wasted..." He stared into his glass as if he could see her at the bottom of its amber depths. "Anyway, the sooner that you accept that, the better off it will be for all concerned."

I glared at the back of Steve's head when he turned to watch the ballgame. "Right. No problem," I groused on my way to fill the drink order ticket Libby was waving at me from the other end of the bar.

I was pretty sure acceptance would come eventually. But absolutely, positively not before I reacquainted myself with the concerned neighbor who called in the "murder." And definitely not before I dealt with the actress in the entryway crooking her finger at me.

What was my mother doing here?

I shook my head and held up the bottle of tequila in my hand. "I'm working," I mouthed, hoping that the biology teacher standing next to Marietta would clue her in to the fact that this wasn't a good time to celebrate her return home.

Libby looked over her shoulder toward the door. "Is that Marietta Moreau?"

The former Mary Jo Digby, pointing at her stilettos like she used to when she wanted me to stand by her side and smile for the cameras like a good little girl? "I'm afraid so."

Libby added lime wedges to the two margaritas I set on her tray. "Not a fan, huh?"

"It's not that." I splashed a shot of bourbon into a shaker to make my first whiskey sour of the evening. "I just don't have time—"

"Perhaps you can make a little after you're done there," Barry said, stepping up next to Libby.

Locking gazes with him while I squeezed a lemon, I received the very clear message that any answer in the negative wouldn't be in my best interest. "Perhaps."

"Want me to get Eddie?" Libby asked as if she could also sense that some trouble was brewing.

More likely, she didn't want to sacrifice her tips because there wouldn't be anyone behind the bar to keep the liquor flowing.

Either way, I knew that I needed some backup to deal with this unexpected family visit and gave her a nod.

I turned to Barry. "Want a drink? It might be a little while."

Stifling a yawn, he looked like he'd rather crawl into bed and pull the covers over his head—which, after his whirlwind trip to do the red carpet gala thing with my mother, was completely understandable. But Barry Ferris, standing here and acting the part of the dutiful stepfather instead of heading straight home from the airport? Not so much.

He waved me off. "I'll let your mother know that you're coming."

I thought of a few other things he could let her know about on my behalf, like respect for other people's time, but kept my mouth shut. Better that I deliver that message myself.

That was precisely my plan when Eddie stepped behind the bar to relieve me and asked, "Is there a reason your mother is pacing in the lobby? She should know by now that she's always welcome here."

The only reason she'd deign to step a toe of her stiletto inside a bowling alley's watering hole would be because she wanted something. Unfortunately for me, something only I could give her.

"We could even promote your mom's appearance and make it an event." Dispensing seltzer water into a glass, Eddie's grin lit up his face. "I know! We could have a mother/daughter night."

"You could feature girly drinks half off," Steve chimed in. "Bring in some guys as servers. I could put in a word at the gym. I'm sure I could find a few boys who'd be willing to oil up and—"

"This is not happening, so stop helping." I glared at him as I stepped out from behind the bar.

"Is that a definite no?" Eddie called after me.

"That was a definite *no way*." Working my way through the crowd, I intended to bring tonight's mother/daughter event to an equally rapid conclusion, but Marietta was nowhere to be seen in the lobby.

Barry pointed me toward the ladies' room. "She stepped in there for a moment."

I pushed the door open and found Marietta inspecting her makeup in the oval mirror over the pedestal sink. "About time."

I was really tired of people saying that to me this week. "You realize that I'm working here tonight, right?"

She cast a glance at my reflection in the mirror. "Sorry, I know we're interrupting, but you didn't reply to my text and—"

"Like I said, *working.*"

"I know, I know. So I'll make it fast." Turning to face me, Marietta's green eyes sparkled. "A little bird told me that you saw a certain movie this afternoon."

Criminy, this was about her movie? "Yep. And as I'm sure you already heard from Gram, we thought you were awesome, especially in that death scene."

She beamed. "Did you really think so?"

I was the only one of the two of us in the bathroom who knew I had just told a whopper of a lie, so there was no upside in providing an honest critique of her overly dramatic sixteen minutes of screen time. "Absolutely. Your makeup looked good too. You really looked dead."

A little frown line between her brows stretched as far as her latest Botox injection would allow. "Honey, I felt close to dead after all those takes with that wretched pillow over my face. I swear," Marietta said, dropping into the Tupelo honey-sweet accent she adopted back in the 1980s for her TV show. "That boy was takin' way too much pleasure in silencing his mama."

I kept my mouth shut. She had set me up for too cheap of a shot.

Reaching out, she took my hand. "But that's not why I'm here. Your grandmother also mentioned the very sweet welcome-home soiree you two cooked up."

For a little bird, Gram had done a heckuva lot of chirping over the last couple of hours. "I thought that was supposed to be a—"

"A surprise, I know. But once she told me how early I needed to be there, I knew that something was up."

Gram also insisted upon a celebration every time Marietta scored a role in a movie or TV show, so the surprise factor of this party was doomed from the start. "Five o'clock isn't *that* early." Surely, she could manage to be up and in full makeup regalia by then.

Marietta rolled her eyes. "Actually, she told me four o'clock. Probably to make sure I was there on time."

That sounded like Gram, but the sly smile hanging from my mother's blood-red lips told me that there was more to this story.

"I assume that you'll be there even earlier to help with the preparations for the festivities," she said.

I hadn't planned to, especially since I wanted to spend the bulk of the day chatting with Naomi Easley's neighbors. "It's a barbecue so there's not a lot of prep work to do, but I should be there by four. That will give me plenty of time to—"

"Could you make it closer to three?" Marietta's cheeks flushed with more excitement than this family gathering warranted. "I have something I'd like to talk to you about."

The last time she said that to me, I ended up moving into her husband's house. Since I was already in the rental house of her choosing, and I was dating the guy who had passed her "mom" test when she asked him about his intentions, I could only guess that she had some news that she wanted to share. "Something that you can't tell me now?"

"Contrary to what you may believe, I do listen."

Only when she had to, but okay.

"So now is not the time because you need to get back to…" She flicked a bangled wrist toward the door. "Whatever it is that you do at this establishment."

I bit back a sigh. "I'm just helping out."

"Because, sugar, if it's more than that and you need the money—"

"I don't." I did, but I wasn't about to admit it so that she could reprise her recent role as Port Merritt's biggest spender. "It's just while my friend Roxanne is on maternity leave."

Marietta pressed her warm palm to my cheek. "I'm sure it is," she stated in a mocking sing-song tone.

Enough.

I needed to end this before I said something I'd regret, and held the door open to get her feet moving. "I'll see you tomorrow. Is there anything special that you want on the menu?"

My mother gave my cheek one last caress before she sashayed into the lobby. "My darling, I do believe that the plan for tomorrow is perfect just the way it is."

Watching her sidle up to Barry, I had no reason to doubt the truth behind her words. But I had a niggling feeling that we weren't talking about the same thing.

Chapter Twelve

"You're right on time," Mavis Burnside said, giving me a quizzical look while holding her door open wide for the black plastic shampoo bowl in Donna's hands.

"And I brought reinforcements." Donna headed straight for Mavis's older sister, who was sitting in the center of a three-cushion sofa with a ginger tabby cat on her lap. "Hello, Althea. It's nice to see you today. You remember Charmaine, don't you? Eleanor's granddaughter?"

Donna had clued me in that she was going to introduce me to Althea Burnside Flanders immediately upon our arrival at the condo she had been sharing with her sister since losing her husband last winter.

Fine by me. In case anyone happened to mention my visit to a certain detective who might return with some follow-up questions, I wanted both Burnside sisters to think of me as Donna's pal. As opposed to the county employee who had no business standing in the middle of their living room.

The wrinkled brow under the gray fringe of bangs indicated that Althea didn't recognize me any more than her cat did, but she nodded just the same. "Oh, yes. Long t-time, no see."

I wasn't so sure that Althea believed the words that had been some struggle for her to get out. However, she was quite right. It had been over eight months since I'd seen the former piano teacher.

"Nice to see you two again. Donna's letting me tag along today." I held up the coil of spray hose I'd carried into the condo as if it could splash a little legitimacy on my guest appearance. "She also seems determined to put me to work, but I promise that I won't get anywhere near a pair of scissors. I just get the pleasure of watching her do her thing, if that's okay with you."

Althea cocked her head, confusion clouding her watery blue eyes. "I don't think I understand. Are you going into the b-business, honey? Is that why you're here?"

The part of this nice old lady's brain that controlled her speech may have been damaged, but her ability to recognize a flimsy excuse when she heard it seemed unimpaired.

I laughed her off and pointed at my ponytail. "No, I can barely style my own hair. I just happened to be in the area," I said, mentally kicking myself for veering off the script I had gone over with Donna on our way over here.

Donna's eyes widened as if I had just lobbed a grenade into the tool bag slung over her shoulder. "And I invited her to join our girls' beauty day because ..." She signaled with a little nod that I'd better fill in the blanks before that grenade exploded in both our faces.

"I do nails!" I said, blurting out the first thing that came to me.

Doing a double-take, Donna choked back a snicker. "She does nails—but apparently only on Sundays, so I thought you ladies might enjoy getting manicures."

Althea lifted the hand that had been stroking the tabby's fur and inspected her nails. "I haven't had mine done in…forever. Probably not since all the…trouble."

Trouble? I turned to Mavis.

"With her dementia getting worse, that's what she's been calling everything bad that's happened since Harold died," she whispered in my ear.

Without missing a beat, Mavis picked up the cat from her sister's lap and set it on an embroidered throw pillow. "Then it's high time we treat ourselves, don't you think, dear?"

"That depends on…how much it costs," Althea said, shooting me a none-too-subtle wink.

I couldn't help but smile at the woman who obviously still knew how to negotiate to her advantage. "All it will cost is a little conversation. I haven't seen you in such a long time, we can fill one another in on all the latest news."

Mavis grinned. "I'm pretty sure Charmaine means the latest gossip."

Althea extended her arm to be helped up from the sofa. "I'm in."

While Mavis guided her sister to the chair in front of the shampoo bowl that Donna had set up in the kitchen,

I hurried ahead with the hose.

"You do nails?" Donna leveled her gaze at me. "That's seriously the best you could do?"

"It's all I could think of. You have your little manicure kit with you, right?" I asked with the hope that this mobile salon side-business of hers was a full-service one.

"Of course." She pointed the spray nozzle at the tote bag slung over one of the chairs in the adjacent nook. "I also have a few bottles of polish in there."

"You're the best." Because all I had in my tote was an emery board.

"Speaking of the best," Donna said as she aimed a happy smile at Althea slowly limping toward her with the assistance of a cane. "Look at you go. That physical therapy is really paying off."

Althea grunted, her brows knit with determination while maintaining a white-knuckled grip on that cane. "Some payoff."

Following like a mom shadowing a baby learning to walk, Mavis helped her sister lower herself into the chair. "Don't dismiss your progress. You're able to make it clear around the block now. We couldn't say that the last time you were here," she said to Donna.

Donna draped a black cape over Althea. "That's awesome. So what shall we do today? How about some pink streaks to celebrate the new you?"

Althea grunted again. "That's for girls…your age."

"Age is just a state of mind, honey," Donna said while she turned on the water.

Apparently satisfied that her sister was comfortable,

Mavis took a seat at the table where I had set up my manicure station. "My knees might disagree with that statement, but I'd like to believe."

"So would I." I took her right hand and inspected five fingers that looked like they hadn't seen a professional manicurist in months. Given the caregiver role this retired nurse had taken on, it came as no surprise.

She leaned in while I reached for the clippers. "You're what? All of thirty-three or thirty-four?"

"Thirty-five." With a biological clock ticking a little louder every day.

"You're a baby."

No, I wasn't, as that ticking clock kept reminding me. Because if I wanted to have a baby, I needed to do something about it.

Not that I was in any better position for that to happen than when I was married to Chris.

"Are you okay, Charmaine?" Mavis asked, pulling a curtain over the image my brain had conjured of Chris as a new dad.

I looked up from the thumbnail I was trimming. "Sorry, I was just thinking about…" Anything that would divert her attention elsewhere. "Actually, what brought me to your neighborhood today: the condo for sale across the street."

Mavis nodded as if a light bulb had gone on over her head. "Oh, the open house."

There was an open house today? Perfect!

"I thought I'd check it out for the lady who lives next door to me. She's been talking about downsizing for a while." Which was true, but in the context of moving to Colorado to be near her grandchildren, not across town. "So she might be interested."

"You might want to mention that someone died there." Mavis's fingers tensed. "You know about that, right?"

Did I ever.

"I heard about it from my grandmother." And a few other people.

"The way news travels around here I imagine most everyone's heard. I figure that's the main reason it hasn't sold."

"What?" Althea called out from fifteen feet away while Donna snipped at the nape of her neck.

Mavis glanced back over her shoulder. "We're just talking about Naomi's place across the street."

"No buyers for it yet, huh?" Donna asked.

"Not yet." Mavis shrugged. "At least not that I've heard about."

"What about that…guy?" Althea chipped in.

Mavis turned to face her sister. "What guy?"

Althea had a look of victory on her face, clearly pleased that she had remembered something that her sister hadn't. "The…tooth…" She shook her head while her lips worked to pry open the file where the word she was searching for used to be stored. "That *tooth* guy."

"Do you mean that dentist?" Mavis asked.

What dentist?

Althea nodded, making her head a moving target for Donna. "We saw Dr.…what's his name…on our walk."

Mavis turned back to let me finish shaping her nails. "She's confused. She thought she recognized her dentist, but that was weeks ago."

"Oh wait. I-I remember now," Althea stated as if she had to prove to herself and everyone in the kitchen that her damaged brain didn't make her any less reliable as a witness. "He was making a house call. With that tree guy. Probably the jerk that c-cut down my plum trees."

Mavis shook her head and murmured, "Not again with the trees."

"A dentist and a tree guy?" Donna looked in my direction as if she needed a translator.

She wasn't the only one, although I had noticed some skinny tree stumps in the narrow stretch of lawn that bordered their neighbor's driveway.

"Someone cut down her trees?" I whispered while Althea struggled to explain the mystery of the missing trees to Donna.

Mavis blew out a weary breath. "It's something that I guess had to be done because they weren't the ornamental plum trees like Harold thought. Anyway, when the neighbors complained to Naomi about the fruit making a mess on their driveway—"

"Naomi? Why complain to her?"

"She was in charge of the grounds committee for the complex. I know she felt horrible about it, because the service she called came out to whack the trees a week after Harold's funeral. Althea was here, mending from a broken leg, crying, yelling at Naomi for killing her trees every time she came over to visit." Shoulders slumped,

Mavis stared at the fingernail I was buffing. "Eventually, her dementia will steal away her memory of what she's been calling 'the trouble.' In the meantime, almost every man she sees in the neighborhood is suspected of being a 'tree guy.'"

"You have to w-watch for 'em," Althea stated emphatically as if she had overheard us. "Riding around in their vans, trying to…drum up b-business."

Mavis schooled her features with patience. "I don't think that's something you need to worry about, honey."

"I know what I saw," Althea protested. "A white van."

Donna bent down in front of Althea to trim her bangs. "Maybe it was that dentist's van with all his equipment. That's a possibility because he'd need to pack a lot of stuff for house calls, right?"

Althea shrugged. "Maybe."

"I don't know what she thinks she saw," Mavis muttered. "But I'm quite certain it wasn't a mobile dental clinic."

I pushed the three bottles of nail polish to the center of the table for her to choose a color. "So no van, huh?"

She pointed at the clear gloss. "Not that I noticed. Of course, at the time, my main focus was on keeping her upright."

While I brushed on a glossy layer of aromatic polish to Mavis's thumbnail, I tried to think of a way to return to the subject of Naomi Easley's drowning. "But *you* saw these two guys at the condo across the street?"

She nodded.

"Think they were interested in buying it?"

"I doubt it. It wasn't for sale yet."

I dipped the applicator into the bottle. "When was this?"

"The day that Naomi died."

Chapter Thirteen

"And I'm sure your neighbor would find this spacious bathroom to her liking," Bonnie from Durand and Terry Realty said, giving me a tour through Naomi Easley's condo. "You'll note the grab bar for security getting in and out of the soaking tub."

Not that it helped Naomi any that last night.

Bonnie cleared her throat as if the petite sixty-something had read my mind and pointed the toes of her nutmeg leather flats in the opposite direction. "Moving on, across the hall we have the spare bedroom and the lovely garden view."

"Very nice," I could say with all honesty as I imagined Naomi's final days here. The interior was a little worse for wear, but new carpeting and some updated fixtures, along with a warmer color to replace the eggshell white on the walls, could make this duplex very inviting.

If you didn't think about the last person to soak in that bathtub.

After showing me the master bedroom at the end of the hall, I followed Bonnie back to the kitchen where she handed me a flyer from a short stack next to a coffee mug full of pens.

"This also has my number if she'd like to schedule an appointment." Her mauve-tinted lips stretched into a bright smile worthy of a toothpaste commercial. "The condos here typically go fast, so if she's really interested, she shouldn't wait too long, if you know what I mean."

I knew exactly what she meant. But since this condo was listed because of an atypical circumstance, I also knew that it wouldn't be the one selling like hotcakes.

"So those two gentlemen who looked at the place a while back didn't make an offer?" I asked after helping myself to an ergonomic grip pen.

Bonnie seemed to downshift into neutral. "I'm sorry. I'm not at liberty to discuss other offers."

More accurately, there were no other offers, and she couldn't help me identify Althea's "guys."

"No problem." I had figured it was a long shot, but at least this open house provided me the occasion to check out the scene of the alleged crime. And come away with a pretty nice pen.

I was thinking about all the identical pens Naomi had collected when I noticed Leland Armistead waving some long-stemmed blooms at me from behind the hydrangea bordering his driveway.

"I thought that was you getting outta that car a couple hours back." He pointed at Donna's Mini Cooper with his pruning shears. "Canvassing the neighborhood, are you?"

"Not exactly," I said as I approached. *So please don't*

tell Steve that if you happen to see him. "I was just chatting with the ladies across the street."

Zeroing in on the real estate flyer in my clutches, he nodded with approval. "And takin' the opportunity to get another look at the scene, I see."

This little old dude was too observant for my comfort level.

Which meant that he was exactly the man I needed to help me fill in a few blanks. "Actually, I went in to chat with Bonnie, the real—"

"The agent who's havin' a heckuva time finding a buyer for the place? Oh, I know. She's bemoaned to me plenty that all she's gettin' are curiosity-seekers."

And just had one more.

"That's probably to be expected," I said, tucking the flyer away in my tote and grabbing my notebook. "We'd all like to understand what happened that night."

"Indeed we would." Leland's eyes gleamed with anticipation as I poised my new pen over a fresh page. "Rest assured, I made every effort to be an open book when your nice detective interviewed me, but if there's some additional information that I can provide…"

"Actually, there is. The ladies across the street mentioned seeing a couple of men at Naomi's door earlier that afternoon. Althea thought there might be some connection with a tree trimming service."

"My dear, Althea thinks every stranger in the neighborhood is here to cut down another one of her trees."

"I understand that the tree incident was very upsetting for her."

"*Upsetting* doesn't do justice to how she felt. I told Naomi that she should have rescheduled, but..." Leland lowered his voice. "I don't like speakin' ill of the dead, especially out in the open where everyone can see us. So perhaps you'd like to come in where we can have a more *private* discussion."

Indeed I would.

Two minutes later, I was sitting in a cushy floral-patterned armchair when Leland handed me a tall glass of iced tea with a sprig of mint. "Are you sure I can't offer you some pound cake? I made it yesterday. My mama's recipe." He fixed a loving gaze at the framed picture of Jerome on the table next to me. "A family favorite."

"Sounds great." It also sounded like this nice man was hungry for companionship after the death of his partner. "But I have to pass." And save my calories for the welcome-home party that I was going to be late for if I didn't move our conversation along.

I took a sip of very sweet tea and set my glass on the ceramic coaster next to Jerome. "You were telling me that you discussed the tree situation with Naomi."

Leland eased into the padded pine rocking chair six feet away. "I told her that she should wait, but that head-strong woman refused to budge. Said that she had to enforce the community rules." He slanted me a glance as he raised his glass to his mouth. "They're very big on rules around here. Sticklers about schedules, too. Unfortunately."

"Unfortunately? Do you mean the scheduling of that service?"

Swallowing, he slowly nodded as he rocked. "Cuttin' those trees down changed everything around here. Made enemies out of what had been pretty friendly neighbors and gave Naomi the reputation of being a merciless enforcer."

"That couldn't have been fun," I said, scribbling a note about Naomi, the neighborhood enforcer and killer of trees.

"No, and I'm quite certain that things were said in the heat of the moment that she didn't mean."

I stopped scribbling. "She who? Naomi?"

"Oh, no. Althea. Don't let the fact that she sits docilely with Naomi's cat on her lap fool you. Althea's got quite the mouth on her. Just not the vocabulary she used to have. Anyway, I imagine that her only memories of that day are the ones preserved by the pain that's still swirling around in that brain of hers."

I wasn't sure what he was telling me. "The pain of her plum trees being chopped down?" That seemed a little melodramatic.

He looked at me as if I were slower than molasses. "The pain of losing her husband—probably the one constant in her life, helping her keep her memories alive." He took another peek at his late partner's picture. "It was a devastatin' loss that changed everything. Then she fell and lost her mobility right before Naomi chopped down her trees. The woman might as well have chopped Althea's legs out from under her, 'cause I'm pretty sure that's how it felt."

"You don't think that—"

"Althea had anything to do with the drownin'? Nah. She didn't want that cat that bad." Leland shot me a good-humored grin, but the white-knuckled grip he had on the rocker's armrests suggested that he had yet to settle the matter in his own mind.

"Did Naomi ever indicate she was concerned that the situation with Althea might escalate beyond words?"

Leland's expression softened, smoothing some of the lines from the roadmap on his face. "Don't think that was of much concern. Not at the pace the old gal moves. And, of course, Mavis was there to act as peacemaker."

He had a point there. Plus, Mavis watched her sister like a hawk. But even hawks had to sleep sometime.

Hearing my phone ding with a message, I figured Donna was ready to leave, so I scanned my notes to see if I had any unanswered questions. That's when I noticed I had circled *white van*.

I knew it would be a long shot but... "Back to the tree service Naomi called to cut those plum trees, do you happen to remember what kind of vehicle they drove?"

Leland gave me an assessing once-over prior to taking a sip of tea. "I do believe that you'd only ask me that question if it had something to do with the vehicle someone saw in the area that day."

Once again, this Southern gentleman was proving himself to be keenly observant. "That's a definite possibility."

"I knew it. And it was a blue pickup, an old one with a

dent in the driver's side door. No lettering so I can't help you with the name of the company, but I'm sure Florence Spooner, who took over as grounds committee chair, can provide that to you." He flashed me an impish grin. "How'd I do? Did the description match?"

Nope. "You did great. Thanks so much for the good info." I took a long drink of tea and pushed out of the chair. "One last thing before I go. Did you see anyone coming or going at Naomi's place that Sunday prior to you and Mavis letting yourselves in?"

Leland's grin vanished. "Your friend with that cute little car arrived around noon, same as today. Went to Althea's place first and then to Naomi's. Can't tell you when she left because my nephew came over with the kids to take me out to lunch."

"You didn't see anyone you didn't recognize later in the day? Or a strange vehicle or two in the visitor parking area?"

"Can't say that I did." He stopped rocking. "But both Althea *and* Mavis said that they saw someone at Naomi's door that day?"

I nodded.

"Hunh. I wonder who it could have been."

Me too.

Chapter Fourteen

After dashing home to change into a black wrap dress that I accessorized with the citrine and onyx necklace my mother gave me last Christmas, I swished on some mascara and called it good enough if I wanted to make it to Gram's by three.

Knowing a mother/daughter chat would commence as soon as I stepped through the door, I dreaded getting out of Gram's SUV. Especially after I tilted the rearview mirror to apply some lip gloss and saw the orange citrine crystals around my neck aglow like little jack-o'-lanterns.

"Swell." I looked like I'd overdressed for a Halloween party. But since I needed to tell Steve about the two men who had been witnessed at Naomi Easley's condo, my costume was the least of my concerns today.

At least I had finally found an opportunity to wear the art deco necklace that Marietta's stylist had reportedly described as the jewel of her holiday shopping junket. And I didn't hate it. It was just more my mom's style than mine, as was most everything she had insisted upon buying me. Although I did like the dining room table set she surprised me with last year. I hadn't realized she'd had a practical streak in her. Maybe she was finally, at long last, getting to know me beyond the image some publicist had crafted of me for her bio.

The notion filled me with a glimmer of hope that I wasn't walking into a situation that would make me want to pull out the hair I should have spent more time flat-ironing.

"And pumpkins will fly," I said as a parting shot to my reflection, because there was a car I didn't recognize parked on the street out front, right behind an ice-blue Subaru.

Unfortunately, I did recognize that one.

"What's going on?" I asked Gram, who greeted me at the back door with a glass of Chardonnay.

She pressed the drink in my hand as if I was going to need it. "I'd like to state for the record that I had nothing to do with it."

Swell. My afternoon was boding worse by the second.

"Is that mah baby girl I hear?" Marietta called out, shuffling into the kitchen in a pair of gold rhinestone stilettos, followed by Renee Ireland, who was aiming a camera at us as if it were Oscar night.

What the heck?

In need of a diversionary tactic, I looked at Gram, but the only help she offered was to take back the wineglass a second before impact. "I'll hold this for you."

While my mother crushed me against the double Ds barely restrained by the plunging lace bodice of her pink lemonade jumpsuit, I whispered in her ear, "Why is there a reporter here?"

"She wanted to do a little feature on us for the paper."

"Us?" Who did she mean by *us*?

Marietta tightened her jasmine-infused embrace. "Sort of a human interest story that contrasts the mother I played in the movie with the mom I am in real life."

That sounded like more spin from her publicist, and I saw no good reason for me to participate in Marietta's latest fiction. "You played a meddling alcoholic your son hated so much that he killed you. That's hardly a fair compar—"

"Doesn't matter. The point being that it showcases my costarring role. Now, be a dear and smile for your mama," Marietta whispered, posing cheek to cheek.

Like a jungle cat stalking its next meal, Renee worked in silence for several seconds. Then she lowered her camera, giving me the look I used to get from Chris whenever he brought up the subject of trying out for a food channel show.

Will you at least try to look supportive?

"Wonderful," she said, her critical gaze suggesting that I was anything but. "Now, how about a couple of shots where you look relaxed and happy to see one another?"

Renee wanted me to look relaxed? I'd be happy to oblige... in another room with that drink while she and my mother finished their photo shoot.

"How's this?" Marietta asked, hooking her arm through mine as she struck another pose.

Pasting a smile on her face, Renee aimed her camera

at us. "Okay, look happy, happy."

"I am happy, happy," repeated the only one of the two of us having a good time. "I'm back home where I'm surrounded by mah loved ones. What more could I possibly want?"

Better buzz for her performance in *Loving Lucian* so that we could dispense with this command performance in front of the camera?

The little smirk teasing the corner of Renee's mouth told me that she'd also had all the phony southern-fried charm that she could stomach for one afternoon.

"Okay, I think I have everything I need. In here, that is," Renee added as if she were giving the actress next to me a directorial cue.

"Then, let's get a few shots out front. As you suggested earlier, the greenery of mah mama's lovely garden makes the perfect background. Besides, it's a beautiful day. It's a shame to waste it inside."

Since when did my mother want to sink the heels of her slingbacks into Gram's front lawn?

Easy answer. Never.

Something was up—something that explained the apprehension lurking behind my grandmother's trifocals.

I'd like to state for the record that I had nothing to do with it.

Whatever *it* was, I was quite sure I wouldn't be "happy, happy" when I found out about it.

"I don't think you need me for that," I said, exiting stage right to let the resident actress fly solo for the remaining moments of this act.

Just as I was about to reclaim my wineglass, Marietta grabbed my hand and pulled me toward the front door. "Sweetie, you couldn't be more wrong."

With Renee looking like the cat that ate the canary while she held open the door, I scanned the yard to see if she had arranged for some of Marietta's fans to spring out from behind the bushes.

But there was nothing and no one that appeared to be out of place.

Except for that car out front I hadn't recognized—the pearly white one that looked almost identical to Renee's Subaru.

As we stepped off the wooden porch, Marietta held fast when I angled past one of the azalea bushes edging the walkway.

"Let's avoid the grass, shall we?" she said, tugging me to her side.

I glanced back at Renee, who was following with a tote bag slung over her shoulder as if she planned to make a getaway after this last shot. Something I envied her for. "I thought you wanted some pictures in the garden."

"I think there's a good spot up near that tree," she said.

In the shade of that thirty-foot dogwood? I was no pro in front of the camera like these two, but even I knew we would need good lighting if they really wanted to use any of these pictures in the newspaper.

When we reached the low hedge in front of that tree and Marietta flashed her chemically whitened teeth at me instead of Renee's camera, I failed to see what she was waiting for. "Now what?"

My mother wiggled her index finger to indicate that I should take another look at that white car.

That's when I saw the new-car sticker on the window and all the air left my body as if I'd been sucker-punched. "Please tell me you didn't..."

"Surprise!" Marietta squealed, wrapping her arms around me while Renee clicked away, capturing the moment.

It was everything I could do to keep from screaming. "What is this?"

"Your grandmother mentioned that you needed a new car, so I thought why wait?" Marietta swept a graceful hand past the right taillight as if she were filming a car commercial instead of advertising how generous a mother she was. "Merry Christmas a couple of months early, mah darlin'!"

Renee sprang in front of me like a card-carrying member of the paparazzi. *Click click.*

"Thanks, Mom," I said to fulfill my role as the dutiful daughter. But once the camera that I wanted to stomp into oblivion wasn't around to influence our performances, she was going to hear exactly what I thought of the fiasco she had sucked me into.

Gram stepped between us like a referee trying to maintain order at a boxing match, and gave me a coaxing nod. "What a pretty car, don't you think, Char?"

I glowered at her. *Don't try to make nice. You got me into this mess.*

She gave me the *look* a split second before turning to

my mother. "Yes, indeedy, and I love the color. But when did you have time to go car shopping? You just got back home."

Marietta smiled at the reporter tucking away her camera. "After we made the arrangements for today's interview, I just happened to mention that I wanted to surprise Chahmaine with a new car, and Renee was nice enough to help me out."

I bet.

"The assistant manager at the dealership is my neighbor," Renee explained to Gram. "Always gets me a great deal, so I made a suggestion to Marietta as to what I thought Charmaine might like and..." She aimed a victory smile at me. "Here we are."

And here she was to tie a bow around the story she had helped create. Such a great deal, indeed.

Renee handed me a business card. "If you decide you'd like a different model or color, here's her number. I'm sure she'd be happy to help you find exactly what you're looking for."

"Thanks." But a different paint color wouldn't begin to address the problem I had with this entire *deal*.

"I didn't know she was going to do that," Gram murmured while Marietta walked Renee to her car. "If I'd had an inkling that your mother was going to take it upon herself... Well, I never would've mentioned that your car was in the shop."

"Not your fault." Because this wretched debacle rested squarely on the slender shoulders of the publicity hound walking toward us.

Marietta beamed. "I thought that went exceedingly well."

"You would. Let's go back inside and I'll tell you what I think," I replied, my cheeks burning as I headed for the house.

"I don't understand." My mother's heels tapped behind me like a frenetic metronome. "Don't you like the car?"

Holding the door for her, I locked on her gaze. "You mean the prop?"

Marietta narrowed her eyes as she passed. "Rather expensive to be just a prop, don't you think?"

I slammed the door behind my grandmother. "Well, if that's not the prop in that stage play you just put on, then I certainly am."

"I resent every bit of your inference," Marietta protested without a trace of her fake accent. "I would never treat you that way."

"You just did." Dropping into the brown recliner before Gram decided to claim her favorite chair, I pointed toward the kitchen. "Maybe you could start the coffee," I suggested to my grandmother. "I'll be along in a minute." Or five.

She aimed a tentative smile at me. "I'll find us another bottle of wine, too. Something tells me we may need it."

The second Gram shuffled into the kitchen, Marietta folded her arms and fired off an angry glare from the sofa. "You have completely misinterpreted my intentions."

"Really? You're going to sit there and lie about how

you used me to make yourself look good in the local newspaper?"

Shifting on the sofa cushion, my mother broke eye contact. "You mustn't think of publicity in those terms. I learned early on that to make it in this world, you have take advantage of every opportunity."

"I am not an opportunity for you to take advantage of. I'm your daughter."

"Oh, sweetheart, I wasn't referring to *you*," she said, her voice as soft as melted butter. "I meant your car situation."

"Which you took advantage of to make yourself look good."

"Did you not need a new car?" Her butter-soft tone hardened into a frozen brick. "One that won't break down and leave you stranded in some godforsaken location? Or perhaps I misinterpreted your grandmother's misgivings about that lemon that your ex stuck you with."

"Leave any misgivings that someone might have about my 'car situation' out of this. This is about boundaries, and you just proved that you have no respect for mine."

"Because I want to ensure your safety?" Marietta raised her hands in mock surrender. "Excuse me for trying to be a good mother."

I choked off the laughter bubbling in my throat. "This is about you being a good mother? Come on, we both know this is about you wanting to have the *appearance* of being a good mother. And the next time you arrange for a reporter to catch you in that act, leave me out of it."

She gaped at me as if I had reached across the room and slapped her.

Scrambling up from the recliner before I said anything else that I'd be sure to regret later, I made a quick exit to cool off.

Which might have been in the realm of possibility if Steve hadn't been peering into the window of the shiny new car parked out front.

"Whose car?" he asked, stoking the fire singeing my cheeks.

I reached out for a much-needed hug. "Long story."

"Has something happened that I need to know about?"

I thought about what I found out from the Burnside sisters. "Yep."

"But I take it that you don't want to get into it now."

"Nope." In that moment, I was content to just bask in the distraction of Steve's embrace.

"We could go inside and do this instead of standing in the street."

"My mother's in there."

"Or we could stand in the street and make out," he said lowering his lips to mine.

I was good with that.

Chapter Fifteen

"What exactly do you expect me to do with this information?" Steve asked almost four hours later while I filled Gram's sink with sudsy water.

What did he think? "In light of the fact that these two men were seen visiting Naomi Easley shortly before she got into that tub, don't you think we should find out what they were doing there?"

"*We?*"

"I meant in general, as part of the investigation into her death."

Taking over at the sink, Steve shut off the water. "That investigation is over, as you well know."

"But now you have this new information about these two guys."

"And you think they could shed some light on what happened that night."

Yes! "They could. I know there's not a lot to go on here—"

"Not a lot?" Steve's lips drew into a humorless smile. "There's not even that much."

"But isn't it worth—"

"All the time it would take to find someone who could identify them?"

Steve was making it sound like it would take forever. Sure, it was a long shot, but… "If it could help determine that her drowning was or wasn't accidental, wouldn't—"

"But it wouldn't," he said, handing me a plate to dry. "Even if someone confessed that they held her under, a good lawyer could probably get them off because homicide by drowning is virtually impossible to prove."

"But—"

"Remember, there were no signs of a struggle and she'd been drinking. Once we get the tox results back, we'll know more. In the meantime, do me a favor and find something else to obsess about." He grinned. "That car outside you're so pissed off about should be enough to keep you occupied."

I groaned. "Don't remind me."

"All in all, I thought that went pretty well," Gram announced, coming in from the living room with two empty wineglasses.

My mother wasn't speaking to me, I now had two cars that had come to me at a soul-crushing cost, and Steve had shredded the value of the eyewitness testimony I'd brought him like it was cabbage for the coleslaw I had made earlier.

"It could have been worse." I could have beat Barry senseless with the barbecue tongs when he came out to suggest that I apologize to Marietta.

"You two need to get past this." Gram clucked her

tongue as she set the glasses on the tile counter. "Not even saying good-bye to one another. You should both be ashamed for the way you're acting."

"I didn't start it," I protested, well aware that I sounded like a ten-year-old.

Steve snickered. "Very mature."

I stuck my tongue out at him.

Gram heaved a sigh. "I'm dealing with children here."

"Yes, you are, Eleanor," Steve said, grinning at me.

She slanted him a cool glance. "I was including you."

I was a second away from teasing him about joining me as one of Gram's problem children when she pointed her finger at my face. "While you may not have started this kerfuffle with your mother, you're going to be the one who ends it."

Me! "After what she did today?"

"Sweetheart, I recognize that she was way out of line to use you like that, but one of you has to make the first move."

"I don't owe her an apology." I didn't care how shocked my new stepfather looked when I told him so... in slightly more colorful language.

Gram gave my shoulder a gentle squeeze. "No, but you owe your mother the opportunity to fix this."

Short of going back in time for a do-over so that Marietta didn't have to try so hard to play the good mother, I didn't know that there was any hope in fixing this.

"I mean it," Gram said when I didn't answer.

"Yes, ma'am." I could plainly see she meant every

word she said.

But that didn't mean that I had to agree with her.

✳

Dreams about cars hurtling toward me like in a deadly game of dodge ball kept me tossing and turning until I finally kicked off the covers around three. That's when I got up, picked up a fork, and parked myself in front of my TV with a hunk of the pumpkin cheesecake left over from my mother's party.

Not a smart choice, which my churning gut informed me even before Fozzie licked my plate clean minutes later.

It didn't fix anything.

Not with my mother.

Not with the grandmother who was disappointed in me.

Not with the detective who accused me of being obsessed with Naomi Easley's death.

And maybe I was, a little. I preferred to think of it as giving the unusual demise of one of my grandmother's friends the attention it deserved.

Did my restless mind require cheesecake to provide that attention? Only at three on Monday mornings after yelling at my mother, and even then that wasn't a firm rule because it gave me one more thing to regret.

"Well, today is off to a stellar start," I grumbled to the dog prancing ahead of me to the kitchen. While he made a beeline for his water dish, I ground some beans to make a pot of wake-up juice, since going back to bed would be an exercise in futility.

Fozzie knew that the gurgling sound of the coffee-maker signaled that it was time for me to get dressed and atone for the evils of the prior day, or minute as the case might be. So he met me at the door with his leash and we went on a brisk run in the predawn drizzle.

It didn't take long for us to jog eight blocks south to the front gate of the Victorian that Gordon and Paula Easley reluctantly admitted had once been listed for sale. Since his mother had moved into her condo around the same time, it seemed perfectly logical for her to list the big, dark house I was staring up at.

So why follow my mother's example and put on a show about it?

The only thing that made any sense to me was that they didn't want Gordon's sister to find out just how close she had come to being ousted from her home.

Considering the level of exasperation in Paula's voice when she vented about Robin's unwillingness to help with family matters, I suspected that the "problem" Gram had mentioned had been festering within the Easley clan for a long time.

Did it cause Naomi to second-guess her decision to sell two years ago? Because unless she'd had more money squirreled away somewhere, her big nut of an asset was this painted lady.

Watching a beam of light slash over the weeds in the yard as a car motored past, it looked like the lady was patiently waiting for someone to take care of her. And if

Robin couldn't handle the simple matter of taking a box of her mother's things, I imagined that Gordon would have to take action sooner or later. If his mother's bathtub request was any indicator, my best guess would be later.

But my gut wasn't entirely convinced. Of course, my gut was also full of cheesecake.

Tugging on the leash, Fozzie whimpered as another jogger in a dark hoodie emerged from the thick mist that had been creeping up from the bay like a ghostly fog.

"It's fine," I said, glancing back while he pulled me to the base of a tree he wanted to water. "It's just another runner." Who, unlike me, actually looked athletic as she pumped her arms to sprint toward us.

But why had she broken into a sprint?

With my heart beating the alarm that I shouldn't stick around to find out, I yanked on Fozzie's leash. "It's not fine. Let's go."

"Hey!" she called out as her running shoes slapped the sidewalk. "What are you doing?"

Growling, Fozzie stepped in front of me like a brawler itching for a fight.

The jogger froze in front of the gate. I couldn't see her well in the early morning gloom, but she appeared to be close to my age.

I inched toward the street with Fozzie to get all the contenders in this fight into neutral corners. "We were just out for a run, same as you."

She pulled back her hood and aimed a dark, wary gaze at me that looked almost identical to the occupant of the house. "I didn't see any running. What I saw looked a lot like someone casing the place. We've had a lot of break-ins in the neighborhood over the last year, and if you're—"

"I'm not." And I needed to come up with a good reason why I had been standing out here for the last few minutes. "Someone told me this house was for sale. My dad's in the market for—"

"They were misinformed. It's not for sale."

"Too bad. He loves these old Victorians." Actually, I didn't know anything about my sperm donor's taste other than his preference for young, impressionable actresses. "And this one's a beauty. Are you the owner?"

"Her daughter."

Robin has a daughter?

When I came here Thursday with my grandmother, I had the impression that Robin lived alone. "Did you two just move in?" I wrinkled my nose in an effort to look as disarmingly confused as Althea. "Because I could have sworn I was told that this was the house."

"Nope. My mom's lived here for years."

"Then maybe I'm on the wrong block. Do you know if there's another Victorian with blue trim around here?"

"Maybe, but I'm only in town once a month, so I'm not the best one to ask." She checked the fitness watch on her wrist. "Excuse me, but I have a six o'clock ferry to catch."

"Heading home?" I asked as she stepped through the gate.

"And to work, so I need to go or I'm gonna be late."

Fozzie pushed forward to sniff the ground where she had been standing as if I wasn't the only one of us interested in this mystery daughter.

"Have a good day, and thanks for the info." Because you just told me that you live close to Seattle—an easy distance away if your mother needs you.

Also an easy distance away to keep in contact with the rest of the family, like a grandmother I imagined she would have visited from time to time. Possibly even exactly one month ago.

Chapter Sixteen

"Look who's gracing us with her presence," Duke announced from his early morning post at his doughnut fryer when the kitchen door banged shut behind me. "Didn't get enough of my charm last night?"

My great-aunt Alice slanted her husband of fifty-three years a glare as she measured flour into a stainless steel mixing bowl. "I think she's had enough of your charm to last a lifetime."

She turned her glare on me when I grabbed one of the aprons from the nearby hook. "And since you're here with us, instead of in your bed where you belong, I'd bet dollars to those doughnuts over there that I know why."

Unless they took the scenic route to the cafe and spotted me talking to Robin's daughter, I seriously doubted it.

"It's your mother," Alice said, pursing her lips with disdain.

Okay, I couldn't deny that Marietta played a major factor in why I was up before the birds. "Yes, but—"

"Oh, you don't have to tell me." Alice gave me a

knowing nod when I joined her at her worktable. "Your grandmother spilled the beans on why Mary Jo was giving you the cold shoulder last night."

I wasn't surprised. Gram rarely kept anything from her sister. "So you heard what my mother did."

"That she bought you that car? And then you got all miffed about it because your mom's been spending money like it's water?" Alice rolled her eyes. "Oh, yeah, I heard all about it."

More creative spin. This was a talent that obviously ran in my family.

"Can't say I'm surprised that she didn't take it too well when you told her to knock off the big spender act. Your mom still has a fortune tied up in that Malibu house that she's having trouble selling, right?" Alice asked in a hushed tone as if this common family knowledge was gossip that dared not stray beyond the confines of her kitchen.

"I suppose." Marietta would have shouted it from the Malibu hills if her red-roofed hacienda had finally sold while she was down there.

"It's just her pride." Alice scooped two cups of sugar into her mixing bowl. "You know how she loves to strut around like she's the queen bee. Mary Jo just can't stand to be reminded that she's no queen around here."

"Ain't that the truth," Duke quipped as he dipped a couple of apple fritters into a pan of sugary glaze.

There was no denying this morning's consensus in Duke's Cafe, but that didn't mean that I needed to give them cause to knock my mother down another peg. Instead, I grabbed a bowl to add some banana walnut muffins to today's bakery case selection, and my breakfast menu for later.

"So, what are you gonna do about the car?" Alice asked, pushing her recipe book toward me.

"I'd really like it if my mother would wise up and get her money back, but..." I didn't see that happening anytime soon, and certainly not after the staged show she had produced for Renee's feature article.

"Wise up," Duke chortled, slipping into a gravelly baritone to belt out a chorus about believing in miracles.

Alice groaned. "It's bad enough that the tiff with Mary Jo made the girl lose sleep. She doesn't need you giving her nightmares."

He shot me a glance. "Since she seems to be here to bake, pretty sure that's not what she's worried about."

Duke knew me too well.

"I don't think you need to be too worried about your mother," Alice said as if she were continuing his train of thought. "She always manages to get by."

With the hope that we could let that be the last word on the subject of my mother, I forced a smile and took a minute to melt some butter in the oven behind me before broaching the reason for my visit.

"What do you know about Naomi Easley's daughter?" I asked, reaching for the cinnamon and baking soda canisters at the end of the table.

"Not a whole lot." Alice met my gaze. "Why do you want to know about Robin?"

"Just curious. I happened to run into her daughter

when I was out with Fozzie, and I was surprised to learn that she was in town."

"Oh, Hailey's been visiting pretty regularly, ever since Naomi took that tumble a couple years back. With both of 'em housebound, she even moved back in for a few weeks to help out."

I didn't understand. "Was Robin hurt too?"

Alice gave me a blank look. "Hurt?"

"You said they were both housebound. What was wrong with Robin?"

"The same thing that's been wrong with that girl for years. Panic attacks. Rarely leaves the house. Naomi thought she was getting better, even got Robin to come to lunch here a few times, but ..." Alice shook her head. "Then Naomi took that fall, and that was all she wrote. The only time I've seen Robin since was at the funeral. Looked like she was clinging to her daughter for dear life, too, the poor thing."

That helped to explain the arrangement that Naomi had made with Robin, allowing her to stay in the house— the home that had probably become a sanctuary for her.

"Then Hailey comes to town to help her mom with shopping and stuff?" I asked.

Seating her bowl on the standing mixer next to her, Alice nodded. "Drives her to doctor's appointments and the like. Took over for her grandma after she moved out. Not sure why, since she has to hop on a ferry to get here."

"So she's been doing that for over two years?"

"Hailey must have wanted to give Naomi a break."

"I guess." Or there was some reason why Hailey wanted her grandmother to stay away from the house.

"Do you have any Cap'n Crunch?" Rox asked when she called me at work almost twelve hours later.

Since one of the assistant prosecutors had me digging up information on a former captain of a commercial crab fishing boat, I wasn't sure I heard her right. "Captain who?"

"Cap'n Crunch, the cereal. It's Eddie's favorite and I'm out because I couldn't stop eating it and pretty much every other box of cereal in the house."

"Sorry, Roxie. I think the only cereal I have in my pantry is oatmeal."

She sighed. "Unless you're gonna come over here and bake sugary cookies out of it, I don't want it."

I couldn't help but laugh. "I thought you were done with cravings."

"I am. I don't want the pickles and cream cheese anymore, but lately it's every form of sugar on the planet. Maybe it's because I'm bored out of my mind, so I've been doing a lot more nibbling."

"Do you want some company? I could stop at the store and pick up something for dinner."

"I'd love that, but only if you and Steve don't already have plans."

"No plans." Plus, Steve would surely mention the car parked across from his driveway, and I didn't want to think about that. "So, what are you in the mood for later?"

"Besides Cap'n Crunch, peanut butter, and maple walnut ice cream? Surprise me."

At six-fifteen, I arrived on Rox's doorstep with Fozzie's leash in one hand and a loaded Red Apple Market sack in the other.

"Hope you don't mind me bringing Fozzie," I said while he led the way to the kitchen. "He's been alone all day because Lily has a cold."

Lily was Fozzie's eleven-year-old buddy who took him for a walk every day after school—something we started when I couldn't leave him in my apartment for hours on end. It earned Lily a little money as my dog-walker, and it provided my pooch a much-needed bathroom break. Now, it just gave him some good exercise.

Except for today, so I owed Fozzie a walk as well as the companionship.

"Are you kidding?" Rox asked. "I guarantee you that I'm happier than he is to have the company." With both hands supporting her lower back, she grinned when I pulled out two small containers of Cobb salad from the bag and then dwarfed them with a tub of maple walnut ice cream and two boxes of cereal. "I know what I want for dinner," she said, snatching up the closest box.

Pulling it from her hands, I returned it to the cantaloupe orange laminate counter. "You're having a salad, and then, if you're very good, you can have the yummy dessert I brought you."

She peeked inside the bag and found the jar of crunchy peanut butter. "Be still my heart. Maple walnut and peanut butter with Cap'n Crunch sprinkles."

And I thought I had a sweet tooth. "Are you trying to put yourself into a sugar coma?"

"Hey, at least I'd get some sleep."

"Speaking of which, you should be in bed. Go," I said, shooing her out of the kitchen. "Find us a good movie to watch, and I'll bring in your delicious salad."

Groaning, Rox waddled into the hallway. "Cap'n Crunch can probably double as croutons. You know, for some extra deliciousness."

"I'm going to ignore that as the ravings of a sleep-deprived pregnant woman. Besides, I have something on ice in the car that you're gonna want to save room for."

The opening credits had barely finished running for *When Harry Met Sally* when Rox turned to me. "What exactly is in the car?"

"I'll be happy to show you." Setting aside my salad bowl, I pushed off her queen-sized bed while Fozzie sprung to the door as if he were as eager for dessert as Rox. "*After* you eat two more bites of your salad."

"Hey, who's supposed to sound like a mom here? You or me?"

"Someone needs to make sure you eat something green so that your kid doesn't come out swaddled in sugar."

"At this point I'd be okay with that," she grumbled, glaring at the round belly stretching her "Baby on board" pajama top to the limit. "'Cause it's been feeling like the pregnancy that will never end."

"It will. He just hasn't been ready to make his grand entrance."

"Well, he has six more days to get ready."

That sounded very specific. "What's in six days? A doctor's appointment?"

She nodded. "And if Junior still doesn't want to come out and play, I'll be induced."

"So the big day will be Monday at the latest?"

I got another nod, this one accompanied by a sigh.

"Okay, then! You're in the home stretch now."

"Thank goodness. 'Cause I'm really tired of having to pee every five minutes." Rox grimaced as she swung her feet to the floor. "And my back is killing me."

"Perhaps some pumpkin cheesecake would make you feel better."

Rox brightened. "*Your* pumpkin cheesecake?"

"I made it for my mother's party last night."

"I'm shocked there's any left over."

There wouldn't have been if she hadn't called to save me from raiding my refrigerator as soon as I got home. "Steve's not big on cheesecake, and I'm quite sure my mother didn't have any."

"Is your mom dieting again?" Rox asked, toddling to the bathroom.

"I think she's on the 'I don't want anything prepared by my daughter's hands' diet."

"What's her problem?"

That was a loaded question. "It's a long story that will definitely require cheesecake."

Rox grinned from the bathroom doorway. "Exactly what I'm in the mood for today."

Ten minutes later, Rox was moaning as if all the

cheesecake she'd wolfed down could make a sudden re-appearance. "I can't believe she did that to you."

"Me either," I said, wishing that my fat cells could find some comfort in the last creamy forkful. "The story will run Wednesday."

"You are so screwed."

Screwed? That felt a little over the top.

Embarrassed to be cast as the *lucky* daughter of a rich and successful local celebrity? Yes, definitely.

Angry to be manipulated in this public way by my own mother? Heck, yes.

But screwed? "You mean because I can't tell anybody the truth without damaging my mother's carefully crafted image?" Because I was already all too aware of the trap Marietta had set for me.

Rox scrunched closer to where I was stretched out across the bed. "That, too, which is exactly why you have to keep the car."

I dropped my fork to my plate. "That is *not* going to happen. I refuse—"

"I know, but think about it. The big show she put on when she presented it to you is going to become 'the story' when the paper comes out. Everyone who knows you is going to expect to see you in it. If they don't and that car continues to sit at your granny's, they're gonna know that this was just some publicity stunt by your mother."

"Crap."

Rox nodded. "Like I said, you're screwed."

"I'm screwed," I repeated at the same time that my

phone started ringing.

Stepping into the hallway with my cell phone, I was relieved to see George Bassett's name as the caller ID. Because I wasn't ready to start driving that Subaru. "Give me some good news, Georgie."

"Uh..." he sputtered after a long pause.

"Okay, then give me the not-so-good news."

"I was taking your wheels off and noticed that your pads are *really* thin."

I wasn't accustomed to being told that anything of mine was too thin and tried to wrap my brain around this being a bad thing. "What's that mean exactly?"

"It means you need a brake job. Pads and rotors."

"Seriously?"

"It'll get unsafe for you to drive her this way pretty soon, so it's not just something I'm calling to recommend. I'm telling you as your friend. We need to do this."

Jeez Louise, this was the second day in a row that someone expressed concern for my safety. Only this time it came across as sincere.

Expensive and sincere.

I gritted my teeth. "How much is this going to cost?"

"You're not gonna like this," he said, sounding just like he did on Thursday.

"Just tell me."

He gave me a rough estimate that made me want to scream. "Could be more. You know these old Jags. Everything's special order."

"Yeah." My car was special, all right.

"So is that a yes?"

What choice did I have? "Go ahead and do what you need to do."

"Okay. I'll give you a call when she's done. It'll probably be toward the end of the week."

That meant I had until Friday to come up with two thousand dollars.

I was so screwed.

Chapter Seventeen

Shortly before midnight struck during the New Year's Eve party scene in the movie, I was feeling almost as miserable as Sally while I drowned my sorrows in a bowl of maple walnut ice cream.

Then I bit down on a walnut shell that felt like a nail being hammered into my back molar. "Ow!" I exclaimed, my misery index soaring.

Pausing the movie, Rox joined me in the inspection of the tiny offender in my palm. "What is that?"

"The part of the walnut that you need to stay away from if you don't want to crack a filling, 'cause I'm pretty sure that's what I just did."

While I gingerly felt along the ridgeline of my tooth, she patted my back. "You'd better make an appointment to see your dentist."

The one who had given me that filling had long since retired. "I don't have a dentist."

"You've been back for over a year. It's high time you get one."

"Now who's sounding like a mother?"

She flashed me a satisfied smile. "I've been in training to sound like one for nine months, so get used to me dispensing unsolicited advice. Doesn't mean it's not good advice, because you need to have that looked at."

Good advice that I couldn't afford to take right now. "Who's your dentist?" I asked for future reference.

"Dr. Carpp."

"Carp, like the fish?"

Rox spelled it for me. "And he's gentle. Eddie even likes him, and he's a big baby when it comes to this stuff. So promise me you'll make an appointment."

"I promise." I just didn't promise when.

Less than an hour later, I was back at the Red Apple Market to find something to soothe my now-sensitive tooth when I spotted Mavis Burnside stocking up on the Greek yogurt that was on sale.

"I like the cherry flavor," I said as I reached past her to pick up a container.

Mavis smiled. "We meet again. How are you doing, Charmaine?"

Based on everything I'd heard when I was giving her a manicure yesterday, I thought total honesty could play to my advantage. "Well, I *was* just fine, and then I bit down on something that screwed up my tooth." I held up the carton of yogurt. "So I might be eating soft foods for a few days."

"Oh, you poor thing. Have you been to a dentist?"

I shook my head. "I have to find one. Who do you and

Althea go to?"

"I've seen him just the one time since I moved here." Mavis furrowed her silvery-brown brows. "Now, what was his name?"

"He's the same dentist Althea was trying to remember yesterday, right?"

She nodded.

Good, because he was the local dentist I'd most like to visit.

"It's a funny name," Mavis said, blankly staring at the carton of eggs in her shopping cart. "I associate it with a fish for some reason."

It was a sure bet as to the reason why. "Dr. Carpp?"

"That's it. Dr. Carpp. How could I forget that name?" She gave her head a little shake. "It's moments like these that make me feel like I'm turning into my sister."

Speaking of whom. "Where is Althea? In the car?"

"Oh, no. She'd get into too much mischief in the car. She's at home watching TV."

"Alone?"

"She's fine. Now that she has that cat to keep her company, she's perfectly content if I need to sneak out for a few minutes."

"Really." Not what I had expected to hear. "Kinda sounds like my grandmother. She loves to watch TV with her cat on her lap."

"I swear, getting that cat has been a godsend."

"I'm sure Mrs. Easley's cat was happy to find such a good second home," I said to see what I could find out about how he came to park himself on Althea's lap.

"I don't know how he happened to pick us, but it worked out great."

How could Mavis not know? She was there.

Studying her face I didn't sense any tension. Actually, quite the opposite because Mavis appeared to be relieved. "You don't know how he came to live with you?"

A sad smile curled her lips. "It was such a jumble after Leland knocked on my door that night. I can only assume that after we let ourselves into Naomi's place, we left the door ajar and Tiger snuck out."

"And snuck into your condo?" That seemed unlikely. The few times that Myron had escaped from Gram's house, he wanted to explore for a while and we always found him hiding from us in the yard. Not inside a neighbor's house.

Mavis shrugged a thin shoulder. "I went back home after the police arrived and found that cat on Althea's lap. So she must've gone to the door and let him in."

"Unless he escaped earlier, and managed to slip in when you weren't looking," I said, thinking out loud. "Maybe when those guys were leaving."

"I suppose that's possible. I did have the garage door open when I left to pick up something for supper, so he could have snuck in then. Who knows?"

"You left?" Around the same time that Naomi might have been sinking beneath the water line in her tub?

Mavis's gaze sharpened much like Duke's did when I criticized his coffee. "Just for a few minutes. Fifteen at the most. The Roadkill Grill is really quick."

I'd eaten there plenty of times with Steve when I

wanted to avoid the wagging tongues at Duke's. It wasn't *that* quick. "But you didn't see the cat or anything that looked out of the ordinary when you got back."

She shook her head. "Not until Leland came over a few minutes into our meal. After that, nothing was ordinary."

"I can imagine." What I didn't want to imagine was Althea anywhere near that bathtub, but if she had been left alone for half an hour or more…

"Well, I should get going," Mavis announced, pasting a pleasant smile on her face, but I suspected that the scene playing out in her mind hadn't been any more pleasant than mine. "Don't want my sister to be alone for too long."

"Right." Because there was no telling what could happen.

"Althea couldn't have been so angry about those trees that she went across the street to yell at Naomi some more, and then what?" I asked the dog in the passenger seat next to me.

"She dunks Naomi in the tub, grabs the cat, and shuffles back to her condo before her sister gets home? Fozzie, the woman could barely walk."

He huffed warm doggy breath at me.

"Oh, trust me. I realize how ridiculous this sounds. But Althea had motive." To kill her neighbor to exact revenge for her trees? "Okay, admittedly it's not the best motive ever. And she had opportunity when she was left alone with that key. Although she probably had to use a walker, so she wasn't going to set any land speed records for murder. And she had that darned cat sitting on her lap by the end of the evening. So tell me where I have any of that wrong and I'll drop the whole hot mess."

Fozzie barked, not in response to any of my musings but at the sight of a golden retriever leading his owner out of the dog park I was driving past.

When the barking morphed into a whimper while he pressed his wet nose to the window, I knew exactly what he was trying to tell me.

"Sorry, pal. I know we didn't get in our walk tonight, but it's after dark and the park's closed."

But the sidewalk around the park was well-lit, and after all the junk food I'd consumed today, heading directly home felt like another poor choice. In no hurry to compound my problems, I parked the Honda near the dog park entrance.

Ten minutes later, my brain was busy churning on the mystery of how that cat ended up with Althea when a tall figure wearing a hooded sweatshirt rounded a corner of the park and jogged straight toward Fozzie and me.

He was probably no more menacing than Hailey had turned out to be earlier this morning, but I had once underestimated the danger from an approaching jogger and I didn't want to make that mistake again.

Just as I tightened my hold on Fozzie's leash and was prepared to scream for help from the teenage girls jogging across the street, the guy stepped off the curb, giving Fozzie a wide berth.

Nodding at me as he passed, I got a good look at the

face that had been hidden in shadow: a handsome black face made all the more interesting by the scar on his jawline, made long ago from a pitbull's bite. Intelligence lurked behind a steady gaze that didn't used to miss much. I knew there was a sharp wit back there too. Not because the former Port Merritt High School wide receiver was giving me a glimpse of it as he bounded by like a gazelle, but because Byron Thorpe used to joke around with me and Rox in Mr. Ferris's biology class.

"Hey, Byron," I said to his backside. "No hello?"

He stopped and wiped the sweat off his brow as he turned. "Char?"

"It's been a long time." Plus, I had gained a few pounds, so I wasn't shocked that he hadn't recognized me.

His face splitting into a smile, Byron took a step toward me and then froze when Fozzie started growling.

"My protector." I pulled Fozzie close to give him a reassuring pat. "He'll relax in a minute. He just doesn't know you."

With Fozzie quieting, Byron gave me a quick hug and then backed away with a show of his palms if he needed to prove his good intent to my bodyguard. "Sorry, I'm sweaty."

He was barely sweating, and didn't appear the least bit winded. He just didn't want to get within nipping range of my dog. Given Byron's history with some of the more aggressive members of the species, completely understandable.

"What brings you to town?" I asked, giving Fozzie

enough leash to let him water the base of a tree. "Some family occasion?"

"Sort of. I'm helping my parents negotiate the sale of their house."

"Really? I hadn't noticed a for-sale sign." Probably because Fozzie and I didn't walk any farther south on that street than the Easley house this morning.

Byron aimed an easy smile at me. "That's because there isn't one. A real estate developer approached them a few weeks back and made an offer. Since I'm their financial planner, I got a call." He looked around as if he didn't want anyone to overhear. "And like I said, we're in negotiation."

The last I had heard, Byron worked for an investment firm down in San Jose, so the negotiation had to be reaching its final stages to bring him to town like a closer. "Going well, I take it."

"It's going okay," he said in a cool tone at odds with the flash of dollar signs in his eyes.

"A real estate developer, huh?" I knew of one that had been gobbling up chunks of bay view property in the four-block radius surrounding the park. But he had recently retired.

Byron nodded.

"A local developer?"

"Maybe."

That would be a *yes*. "Your parents' place would be a nice, big parcel. Plus, it's a great location for anyone wanting to live within walking distance of the hospital."

"It's always been a good location. Near the hospital,

near shopping—"

"Of course, if they want to put townhomes or apartments there, they would need more than just your folks' house. They'd need to acquire some of the adjacent property or it wouldn't be worth their investment."

Instead of responding, Byron pressed his lips together as if he couldn't afford to let that information spill out of his mouth.

"Can't imagine that they haven't been knocking on quite a few of the neighbors' doors," I added, inching closer so that I could read him better in the low light.

He glanced back at the empty street behind him, taking a half-step toward his quickest getaway route. "I really can't speak to that."

Because I was getting too close to the truth? With Fozzie sniffing weeds at the fence line, it surely wasn't because Byron wanted to distance himself from my ferocious fur ball. "I also can't imagine that your mom didn't compare notes with the lady next door before she called you."

He shook his head. "You been talking to my mom, Char?"

"Nope. Since she's the savvy lady who does my grandmother's taxes, I would expect her to look for every advantage. Pretty sure that's why you're here."

He met my gaze with a sheepish grin. "I forgot that you could do that truth serum thing. You know it's a little creepy."

I couldn't help but smile. "So I've heard." On more than one occasion from my ex.

"The deal with Cascara isn't done yet, so don't say anything, okay?"

"Cascara is the development company?" I'd seen several of their signs posted in Marietta's upscale Bayview Estates subdivision, but never anything in this part of town.

Byron nodded. "And I hope to get this thing wrapped up this week so I can get back to the office. There's just one person holding things up."

I had a sneaking suspicion that person was an Easley.

Chapter Eighteen

Since a gunmetal gray Ford pickup was parked in front of my house, I wasn't at all surprised to come home and find Steve watching TV on my sofa.

The same couldn't be said for my dog, who charged into the living room, barking his intruder alert.

"Fozzie, no," I called out over his volume.

"It's okay." Steve held out his hand for Fozzie to sniff. "I'd rather have his first instinct be to go on the offense than for him to want to play fetch with the guy who breaks into your house."

"You didn't break in. You have a key."

"He doesn't know that. Huh, mutt," Steve said, wrestling Fozzie to the floor.

Something about coming home to watch my dog expose his belly for a rub from the guy I loved felt a little too domestic. Like we were all playing house, before establishing the rules of the game.

And I wasn't in the mood to play.

I hung Fozzie's leash on the coat rack and headed into the kitchen with my purchases from the store. "Whatever.

You been here long?"

"Not quite an hour. I called to see where you were."

"Sorry, I might have left my phone in the car when we went for a walk around the park."

"This late?"

Everyone wanted to sound like a mother tonight. "*Around* the park, not in the park. And guess who I ran into."

"Byron Thorpe."

"Jeez, good guess."

Steve chuckled as he entered the kitchen with Fozzie hot on his heels. "I met up with him at the Grill when I stopped for a burger."

"It's funny that he didn't mention that, but he was being pretty close-lipped about what brought him to town."

"Something to do with the sale of his parents' house, right?"

Evidently, Byron had been even less forthcoming with Steve than he had been with me. "Right. Located just down the street from Naomi Easley's house, I might add."

Steve vented a weary breath. "Pretty sure that there are at least a dozen houses for sale in town."

"I'm sure there are." I smiled sweetly at him as I put my cherry yogurt into the refrigerator. "I'm just sayin'."

"What, exactly?"

"That it's an interesting coincidence."

"What's more interesting to me," Steve said, reaching past me for a bottle of beer while Fozzie settled at his feet. "Is why, when you have hardly any food in your refrigerator, you only bought a yogurt."

"I have food. There's kale in there and some spinach for a salad."

"Yeah, yum." He twisted off the cap. "What happened to the leftover cheesecake?"

"Roxie called, and I took it over to her place." What was left of it, anyway.

"Oh." Steve leaned back against the counter. "I thought it might have gone to your mother's as part of a peace offering."

I didn't want to talk about my mother. "Our favorite baby incubator has been climbing the walls waiting for that kid to be born. She needed it more."

"Eddie made it sound like what she needs is sleep."

"It's really hard for her to get comfortable. At least this won't go much longer 'cause if Junior isn't born by the end of the weekend, they're going to induce."

"Then no one in that house will get any sleep." Steve shook his head. "I pity them all those feedings and diaper changes already."

I didn't. Maybe because there was a time not so long ago that I would have traded places with Rox in a heartbeat.

But that didn't happen.

And Steve was entitled to feel any way he wanted to about someone else's baby.

No matter how empty his words made my womb feel.

I stepped over Fozzie to take Steve's beer bottle and saluted him with it. "To the sleepless nights that they've been waiting a long time for."

He wrapped his arms around me while I tilted back the bottle. "And to all the things we can do when we're not sleeping."

Which sounded quite inviting until the cold beer hit my molar like a pickax, and I jumped back so fast that Fozzie scampered into the adjoining dining room.

"What's wrong?" Steve asked, frowning at the way I was holding my jaw.

"Nothing. I just have a sensitive tooth."

"Maybe you should see a dentist."

"So I've heard. Rox gave me the name of hers." I left out the part about Althea having the same dentist. Steve wouldn't appreciate how I came to discover that little fact, and I wasn't in the mood to be on the receiving end of a lecture.

"In the meantime, you should probably lay off the cold stuff."

While he reclaimed his bottle I settled back in his arms. "Yep, ice cream is definitely out." Plus, I had already had more than my fill for one evening.

I locked my hands behind his neck. "I seem to be able to handle the hot stuff, though."

The crow's-feet around Steve's eyes crinkled with amusement as he held me tight. "We'll see how much you can handle."

After Steve left around eleven, I stared at my bedroom ceiling for an hour before calling it quits on the notion of sleep and tugging on a pair of sweats.

Springing into action at the sight of me reaching for my running shoes, Fozzie ran up and down the hall, impatiently waiting for me to let him out.

Ten minutes later, he whimpered his growing displeasure with me when I parked across the street from Byron Thorpe's childhood home. Plus, my restless dog was fogging up the windshield.

"I realize this isn't what you had in mind," I said while I cranked up the defrost. "You thought we were going to the dog park. We can do that tomorrow. Right now, I want to see why a developer would be so interested in this area."

Sure, all the houses on this block were close to shopping, and the location would be ideal for anyone who wanted to shorten their commute to the hospital. But that could be said for my grandmother's house, and no one had come knocking on *her* door.

I was pretty sure that was because the Thorpes' Queen Anne–style house perched on an elevated corner lot high enough to look over all the roof lines to the east for an unobstructed bay view.

"That's got to be the major factor," I said, pulling away from the curb. Because the Walkers' house next door with the dormer windows shared the same elevation. Add the Victorian with the blue trim to the mix, along with the two-story shingled house on the corner I was creeping past, and a developer would have almost three acres of prime view real estate.

"Do you know how much money that would be worth?" I mused aloud.

Fozzie curled into a ball, clearly no more interested in the local real estate scene than Steve had been last night.

"A lot." Assuming that everyone on that block would be willing to sell.

"Byron might have some major persuading ahead of him to close this deal." But based on what I observed in Gordon and Paula Easley's behavior last Saturday, I had a feeling Byron wouldn't be the only one in Robin's ear over the next few days.

✳

"Land sakes, girl." Alice squinted at the kitchen clock mounted above a vintage red and white Coca-Cola sign. "It's barely after five. Don't you sleep anymore?"

Tying an apron around my waist, I approached her worktable. "You're the one who used to love to remind me about how the early bird catches the worm."

"You were probably fourteen and late to work every day that summer. You needed the reminder. Now that you don't need to be an early bird, you should probably work on catching another forty winks instead of that worm." She directed that squint at me. "I'm sure those bags under your eyes would thank you for it."

"I'm sure they would," I said, heading to the closest refrigerator for the carton of butter that my great-aunt's chocolate chip cookie recipe called for. "But since I'm here…" And I couldn't stop thinking about what Byron had told me last night. "You might as well get some free labor out of me."

"Your labor ain't free, kiddo," Duke scoffed as he met me back at the table with two steaming cups of coffee in his hands. "This is called paying off your tab."

I smiled at the feisty coot, who loved to rib me about the tab he used to let me run when I was on his summer payroll. "Dream on, old man."

He set the cups on the table and then exchanged glances with his wife, who gave her head a little shake like a baseball pitcher who didn't like the sign from her catcher.

"What's that about?" I asked as I reached for the bag of sugar.

Duke grumbled an expletive worthy of the chief petty officer rank he had held in the Navy. "I'll just ask flat out. The reason you haven't been here after sun-up doesn't have anything to do with that dang fool Miriam and her betting pool, does it?"

"No." Not this week. "I just haven't been able to sleep."

"Told you," Alice said to Duke. "It's her mother messing with her head."

Yes, she was, which seemed to be what my mother specialized in now that she lived in town. But Marietta didn't have anything to do with all the sheep I didn't count last night. "There's just a lot going on."

"What's going on?" Lucille asked, the back door banging shut behind her.

Duke glowered at his longest-tenured waitress as she hung up her coat. "Do you have some sort of listening device on you so that you can butt into every conversation that doesn't concern you?"

Flashing him a smile, Lucille lumbered over in her squeaky orthopedic shoes and took the seat next to me. "Good morning to you, too, Sunshine. Now, since I have a few minutes until I'm on the clock…" She shooed him away with a flick of her wrist. "Scram, so that we girls can have some privacy."

He cocked his head at her. "You need privacy? I'd like to remind you this is *my* kitchen you've got your hiney parked in."

"Okay, mister boss man," Lucille retorted. "If you want to hear about *my* woman parts, stick around. You might learn somethin'."

Duke spun on his heel and started walking. "I'll pass. Don't wanna ruin my appetite."

Alice scowled at his backside. "Don't be a rude old man."

"That's like telling a dog not to bark," Lucille said, giving my shoulder a conspiratorial bump. "At least this one took his bark elsewhere so that we can have a few minutes of peace."

I didn't equate sitting down with the queen of Gossip Central with being the least bit peaceful. However, I had found it to be informative on occasion, and my weary brain longed for this to be one of those occasions.

I pushed the cup of Duke's foul brew in front of her. "Coffee?"

"No coffee for you, huh? And you're here two mornings in a row," Lucille said, spooning sugar from the bag in front of her into her cup. "So, you're not drinking cof-

fee, and we haven't seen you come in to eat for a week."
Leaning against the flour-coated surface, she looked at
me the way Marietta does when she thinks I should exfo-
liate. "And excuse me for saying so, but you look like
death warmed over. You're not pregnant, are you?"

"No!" Sheesh. Why was that always the first question
everyone wanted to ask here?

"Lucille!" Alice chided. "Don't be a busybody."

"Well, something's gettin' her up at oh-dark-thirty."
Lucille fixed her gaze on me while taking a slurp of well-
sugared coffee. "So? What's goin' on?"

I pushed away the bowl with the butter I had been
creaming. "Before I get into it, you two need to swear
that this won't go any farther than this kitchen."

They both nodded.

I pointed at Lucille. "I mean it. 'Cause this could get
me into some hot water at work."

"Fine! I swear." She stared wide-eyed over the rim of
her cup. "So start talkin'."

I wasn't sure how much I could tell these two without
the news of it flaring out of control like a grease fire, but
I needed their assistance if I was ever going to find the
answers I needed. "You know how I help with the fact-
finding when there's been a suspicious death."

Lucille gasped. "Who died?"

"No one. I mean I'm not talking about something that
just happened. But there was a death last month that I
can't stop thinking about because it was so weird the
way she drowned."

Lucille knit her thin, sandy brown eyebrows. "You're

talkin' about Naomi."

I nodded.

"It was pretty crazy to hear about her gettin' liquored up and passin' out in the tub." Lucille's eyes shifted to Alice. "We all thought so when we heard about it."

My great-aunt leaned in. "Here's something I hadn't realized at the time that makes it even crazier. Eleanor told me that Naomi was nervous about that big step into her bathtub. Told the girls that she was afraid of falling again, so it's hard to make sense of her being found that way."

It appeared that my grandmother had neglected to mention one salient little detail to her sister. "And Donna had just done her hair a few hours earlier."

"That's right. I remember Florence saying something about that." Lucille thumbed toward the dining area behind us. "Considerin' how Naomi wouldn't take a step outside on a stormy day without a rain bonnet, that doesn't sound like her at all."

"I know. It's weird, and a lot of what happened that day doesn't seem like it adds up, but since it's been explained to me that it *could* have been an accident..." And since we all knew who would have done the explaining, I didn't need to mention his name.

Alice stared across the table at me. "If it wasn't an accident, are you suggesting—"

"That they drowned her," Lucille proclaimed with an edge to her tone that was as sharp as a butcher's blade.

They? "They who?"

"I swear." She hung her head, the points of her platinum bob brushing the apples of her cheeks. "Since the poor little thing didn't kick after she fell down those stairs, they decided to finish the job."

"Who?!" I wanted to scream.

"Robin and her daughter." Lucille sniffed with disdain. "Although I bet Hailey got talked into going over to snuff out Granny by her mom. There always was some sort of wacky codependency thing going on in that house."

I looked to Alice for confirmation.

"I told you most everything I know yesterday. There were some obvious issues with Robin. Had been for years. That's why she had to move back in with her mom. And then it only got worse after Hailey went away to school. Naomi didn't talk much about it, and I didn't want to pry into their personal business."

Lucille scoffed. "Maybe we should have. Maybe then, Robin and Hailey wouldn't have gone over there to finish the job."

That was the second time she had said that. "Are you telling us that Naomi's fall at her house wasn't an accident?"

"Doesn't sound like you think her drownin' was an accident."

I shook my head.

Lucille leveled her gaze at me. "How many 'accidents' have to happen before you call it like it is? 'Cause, hon, it seems clear to me—she was murdered."

Chapter Nineteen

"Have you overheard anyone talking about a company called Cascara something?" I asked when I spotted Lucille starting another pot of coffee for the early risers who would be coming through the door at six.

"That construction company? You think they have something to do with ..." She looked at Duke behind the grill and then lowered her voice to a stage whisper. "You know what."

I didn't know what I thought other than it seemed like a strange coincidence that they were trying to acquire property on the street where Naomi Easley's daughter was living.

And I wasn't big on coincidences.

"It could be nothing." And it was definitely nothing I wanted to set the rumor mill spinning into high gear about since I didn't want to hurt Byron's negotiations. "I was more curious than anything else."

"Because they're linked to Naomi in some way?"

"I wouldn't say that." *So don't you say it either.* "I think they built my mother's house, and I was just looking into something for her."

Planting a fist at her thick waist, Lucille cocked her head at me. "For someone good at spottin' liars, that's the best you can do?"

It was this morning. "Just let me know if you hear anything, okay?"

"I'll keep my eyes and ears open. You can count on me."

"I'd rather count on her getting some work done this morning," Duke grumbled at me as I went by. "So if you're finished recruiting my employees to help with whatever this thing is you've got going—"

"I beg your pardon. We were simply chatting." I shot him my best innocent smile. "Girl talk, remember?"

"My memory's fine. So is my hearing." The crease between his bushy silver eyebrows deepened. "You're not sticking your nose where it doesn't belong, are you?"

No doubt the man I loved as much as my own grandfather would think so. "Of course not."

He shook his head. "Lucille's right. You're a rotten liar this morning."

After I got to the office and made an early morning appointment for Thursday with Dr. Carpp, I spent the next ten minutes running background checks on everyone I could find who was related to Naomi Easley.

Other than discovering that Gordon had a lead foot with a decades-old history of speeding tickets, I found a big fat nothing on the rest of the family until I ran a search for nine-one-one calls. There had been two, both placed by Robin Easley Kranick.

The most recent was last August, when she reported seeing a prowler trying to break into her neighbor's house. Which didn't surprise me, since it corresponded to what her daughter had said during that confrontation in front of the house.

The other, dated July seventeenth two years ago, summarized the medical response to Robin's call for an ambulance for her mother. At first, the paramedic's report back to Dispatch appeared to be a lot less dramatic than I had expected. Then, I read four words that kicked my heart into high gear as if I'd mainlined a carafe of Duke's coffee: *Victim claims accidental fall.*

Claims? That was a word I would use if I felt I wasn't getting the whole story.

The summary concluded with Naomi being transported to the local ER for treatment.

If anyone else had questioned Naomi about what caused her to fall down the stairs of her home, it didn't make it into any regional database I had access to. So I had nothing else to go on other than a lot of conjecture on Lucille's part that Robin should have been criminally charged with something resembling reckless endangerment.

With the sound of heavy footfalls coming in my direction, I shut down my computer screen before I had to explain what I was doing to one of Ben Santiago's more rotund junior prosecutors.

"Are you available to sit in on a meeting?" Mason

asked when he reached my desk, wheezing as if he had just completed a marathon.

Instead of filing? "You bet. Now?"

"Now."

Mason marched back toward the criminal division, and I trotted to catch up with him. "What's this about?"

"Not sure why you're needed," he wheezed as we approached the conference room next to Ben's office. "I thought this was going to be routine."

Since I was the administrative assistant who had scheduled this morning's witness preparation session with Ben, so had I. That's why, when the door swung open, I wasn't surprised to see a skinny twenty-year-old. But I hadn't expected to see two men the size of Mack trucks bookending him. Nor had I expected Ben to reach for one of the yellow ruled pads on the table.

While Mason claimed the seat opposite the younger bookend, Ben motioned me in. "We should have known better than to start without you, Charmaine."

From prior experience, I knew this to be code for *You're here to tell me if I can rely on this witness*, so I smiled with the knowledge that Ben wanted me to quietly observe and follow his lead.

When I stepped to the table, he turned to the big man with the graying crew cut sitting across from him. "She helps keep me on track."

That was more Odette's job, but if it would keep me off my knees in the file room, I was happy to play along. "I do my best," I said as Ben slid the legal pad and a pen in front of the empty chair to his right.

I figured that was to give me the appearance of functioning as his scribe. More important, it gave me license to plant my butt in the best seat from which to observe Ryan Pollard, one of the key witnesses in a drug trafficking case scheduled for next month.

Ben pointed his pen across the table at the slouching kid with the acne dotting his forehead. "Charmaine, I believe you spoke to Ryan on the phone."

Rising from the black upholstered chair, I reached out to shake his clammy hand. With the close proximity, I was immediately struck that he reeked of flop sweat and cigarettes. "Nice to meet you in person." *Not so nice to smell you.*

Ryan looked as enthused to see me as my ex at our settlement hearing and gave me a tight-lipped nod.

"His father, Brad Pollard," Ben said, indicating the block of stone with the crew cut to Ryan's left. "And brother, Mike."

Since testifying at trial could be a frightening experience, I was accustomed to younger witnesses bringing a parent to these prep sessions for moral support. But Ryan's family members looked more like mob movie enforcers straight out of central casting.

I smiled as I shook their hands.

They didn't. Instead, Mike slanted a look of contempt at Ryan sulking next to him. "Can we get on with this?"

Spoken like a man who didn't want to be here any more than his little brother.

"Certainly," Ben said, keeping his expression carefully neutral as he proceeded to explain what Ryan could expect to be asked by opposing counsel.

With every second that ticked by, I noticed Ryan getting increasingly twitchy. Same with the brother. But it wasn't until Ben mentioned one of the drug deals that took place at the job site where Ryan had been working that he stared down at the table as if he wanted to disappear into the wood grain.

"And you didn't say a word," Mike muttered through clenched teeth.

Ryan sunk lower in his chair.

Mike folded his beefy arms. "I told you to stick with me."

So Mike Pollard was there when that drug deal went down? "What do you do, Mike?" I asked to get a better sense for why he wasn't on the witness list.

"Roofer for Cascara Construction." He jabbed his thumb in his brother's direction. "I'm this one's foreman."

Cascara?! "This happened at a Cascara job site?"

Mike's steely eyes narrowed to slits. "On this idiot's first day."

"How was I supposed to know who they were?" Ryan asked, his voice high and whiny like a petulant child's. "They arrived with the food truck."

Hurling expletives at him, Mike smacked his brother's arm. "You *ask*, you freaking idiot!"

Mike's father pointed a bratwurst-sized finger at him. "Enough! Get out of here so we can get this done."

"I can take Mike to the break room for some coffee," I whispered to Ben.

He nodded. "No need to rush back. We'll find you two when we're done here."

I took that to mean that it was the older brother he wanted me to observe. Again, not what I had expected, but okay.

"If you'll follow me," I said, extending my arm toward the door like a maître d' leading Mike to his table.

Fortunately, the break room was unoccupied and the coffee pot contained some relatively fresh brew.

I pulled out a chair for him, but he glared at as if it came with a trap door before he lowered himself into it.

I pretended not to have noticed. "How do you take your coffee?"

"Black."

"Heights don't bother you, huh?" I asked while I filled two cups to direct his focus on something he'd be more comfortable with.

"What?"

"Being up on two-story houses. That's about, what ... fifty feet off the ground?" Hoping that was a gross exaggeration that made me look dimmer than the partially burned-out overhead fluorescent, I set the cups on the table and took a seat.

The dismissive smirk tugging at the corner of his mouth told me I'd hit my target. "More like twenty."

"Still, that's up there. I sure couldn't do it."

That earned me two seconds of eye contact before his gaze dropped to the bacon grease stain I managed to get this morning on the placket of my green silk blouse.

Yep, you don't think very highly of me.

If it helped him to view me as less of a threat, I was fine with it. "How long have you been doing this kind of work?"

"Pretty much since high school," he said between slurps of coffee.

"And you worked your way up to foreman. That's impressive."

Mike glanced at the door, reminding me of Steve when Marietta won't shut up.

"It shows that the people in charge at Cascara Construction have a lot of trust in you."

"Someone quit and I took his place, that's all."

"I'm sure they wouldn't give that job to just anyone, especially when there's so much work to be done. Just the other day I heard that a project is going to be starting uptown, near the park."

He gave my cup a hard stare as if he'd like me to occupy my mouth with it. "I wouldn't know."

Mike wasn't trying to mask his annoyance with me, so I had no reason to doubt him. At least so far.

"Might just be rumor. The Easleys mentioned that a certain party might be looking at their house since it's such prime real estate."

He gazed out the window without emoting even a sputtering spark of interest.

Okay, he didn't appear to know anyone by the name of Easley and had no knowledge of Cascara's future plans.

I took a sip of coffee to give us both a break from my fruitless interrogation, and noticed that Mike was tapping his cup as he stared into space.

Duke did that when he had a decision to make. He also did it when he was annoyed—his early warning system to the rest of us to cease and desist or prepare for a loud eruption of Mt. Duke.

Since Mike no longer looked like he wanted to swat me like a fly, I set my cup down and smiled across the table at him. "I know this is a difficult situation for you and your family."

"Yeah."

"But your brother is doing the right thing by testifying."

The tapping continued. "I hope so."

"Mr. Santiago is very good. He'll help Ryan know exactly what to expect when he takes the stand."

"I'm sure."

More tapping combined with the rigid set to Mike's jaw told me that he wasn't so convinced.

"Really," I said, waiting for him to meet my gaze. "Your brother will be okay."

The tapping stopped. Instead, he gripped the cup as if he needed it as an anchor. "You don't know these guys."

"They're going to prison. I really don't think—"

"You people have no idea."

"Mike, are you worried about your brother's safety?"

His mouth a grim line, Mike stared into the depths of his cup. "Not if he gets out of town."

"You mean after the trial."

He hesitated a little too long. "Sure."

Criminy. Ben's key witness might bolt. No wonder Ryan was so twitchy.

"What about you?" I asked. "Are you concerned for your safety?"

"Don't expect any of those punks will do anything to me." He shrugged a meaty shoulder. "Other than to try to get me fired."

What "punk" had that kind of pull? "One of those guys is in a management position at Cascara?"

"Hardly."

Okay, I was getting confused. "I don't understand. Who's gonna—"

"Don't worry about it. I can take care of myself." Mike pushed out of his chair and headed for the door. "Thanks for the coffee."

I bolted out of my seat. "I think you should talk to Mr. Santiago before you leave." Because this situation had escalated far beyond my pay grade.

"I got nothing else to say." He pointed down the hall. "Is this the way out?"

"Yes, but—"

"Tell Ryan and my dad that I'll meet them at the car," he said, turning Patsy's head as he stalked by.

"Wait!" I ran to catch up with him. "Mike, you should really talk to..." Then the door swung shut behind him. "Crap!"

Patsy aimed a smug smile at me. "Did your meeting go well, Charmaine?"

"It went swell," I said, spinning on my heel without a second to spare. Because I needed to go back to deliver Mike's message, and then tell Ben that his key witness might be the next one to rush out of this courthouse.

Chapter Twenty

"Ryan's obviously nervous about testifying," Ben replied after I parked myself in one of the black leather chairs in front of his massive desk and provided the blow-by-blow of my conversation with Mike Pollard. "But if the kid isn't going to help himself by telling us who's been threatening him, there's not much we can do beyond what we went over in our first meeting."

I was sufficiently familiar with the witness deposition process to know that a risk assessment would have been conducted, and Ryan Pollard would continue to receive periodic calls from our witness advocate.

"His dad said that he and the brother will keep an eye on Ryan until the trial." Leaning back in his desk chair, Ben removed his horn-rimmed glasses to clean them. "Don't think we can get him better bodyguards than that."

"I guess." Although one of those bodyguards had been truly scared for his brother.

You don't know these guys.

Just thinking about the way Mike looked like he

wanted to take refuge in his coffee cup when he said that gave me gooseflesh. It also made me wonder if Steve might know them.

I had just returned from lunch when my grandmother called to ask me to take her grocery shopping.

I had a suspicion that an ulterior motive lurked behind Gram's request. But it wasn't until almost six hours later, when we were putting away her four bags of groceries, that she pointed to the brand-new white car still parked at the end of her walkway. "What have you decided to do about that?"

I stifled a groan. "I haven't given it a ton of thought."

Gram scoffed. "I seriously doubt that."

I obviously needed to up my game. Hardly anyone who knew me believed a word I said today. "Really. Rox called yesterday and I spent most of my evening with her, so that didn't leave a lot of time for other stuff."

"Then maybe you'd better make some time, because that car can't sit out there forever."

Something that I was all too aware of. "I will."

"Have you spoken to your mother yet?"

"No," I said on a sigh.

Gram echoed my sigh. "What am I going to do with you?"

Was that a multiple-choice question?

She rested her fists at her hips. "Do I have to get your mother over here so that you two can have a conversation?"

Good grief.

"No. I'll handle it." Eventually.

"In the meantime, what's going on with your car in the shop?"

"Now it's getting its brakes replaced."

Her expression softened. "That sounds expensive."

"Yeah."

"Sorry, sweetheart, but is that going to happen soon? Because, while I don't mind being chauffeured to the store, I will need my car back for mahjong Friday."

Dang. "George said it should be ready by then, so no problem."

Gram brightened. "If it's not, you have that nice new car you can drive."

"Right."

"And since you're already here, maybe you'd like to trade cars now."

Just the thought of driving Marietta's "prop car" made my molar ache. "I really don't—"

"Oh." Gram's gaze fixed on the wrought iron wall rack by the back door, where I had hung her car keys. "I forgot. Your mother took the keys with her. You'll have to get them from her when you two have your chat."

Of course I will.

After I got home and took Fozzie for a walk, I returned with a decision made to call my mother to set up a meeting.

Then, instead of calling her, I ate two of the chocolate

chip cookies I had baked that morning, cleaned out my refrigerator, and made a sweep of all the dog-hair dust bunnies I missed the prior weekend. Then, after fifteen minutes on the elliptical to atone for the cookies, I called to check in on how Rox was doing. That's when Steve arrived to a chorus of barking, and I cut the call short.

"Hey," I said, happy for the nice distraction. I gave him a kiss while Fozzie danced at our feet.

"Hey, you." Steve pulled out of my arms to scratch behind Fozzie's ears and then grabbed the living room remote to turn on the flat screen. "Sit and be good. The playoff game's on."

My dog immediately sat and gave me a doggy grin.

"Yeah, you're never that good for me." I pointed at him. "Don't forget who feeds you around here."

"You just need to show him who's boss," Steve said, patting the sofa cushion next to him while staring at the flickering images of the baseball game.

I stepped in front of the TV. "Did you just tell me to sit and be good?"

Looking up at me, Steve grinned. "Not in so many words."

"That's what I thought." I went into the kitchen to get him a beer. "At the end of the inning, I need to talk to you about something."

"It's not more about the Easley house, is it?" he asked, twisting off the cap while focused on the tube.

"No. It's about a case where you were one of the arresting officers."

"You know I can't give you any specifics that aren't in

the public record."

"I don't want any." But that didn't mean that I couldn't give him some. "There's something that's come to my attention that may affect a case coming to trial."

Setting down the beer, Steve slanted his gaze to me. "What are you talking about?"

He muted the TV and I took the next two minutes to fill him in on everything Mike Pollard had told me.

"While Ben doesn't appear to be overly concerned about his witness's safety, the big brother sure was," I said, angling for a better view of Steve's face when he turned back to the game.

He grumbled an obscenity in reaction to the crack of the bat. "It's not like we have the manpower to assign a security detail, Chow Mein."

"I'm not asking for one. I just think it might be worth someone's time to talk to Mike Pollard so that we can get the name of the punks he was clearly worried about."

Steve's head turned on a swivel, his gaze packing as much punch as the star pitcher's fast ball. "*We* don't need any names. Because *we* aren't going to play junior investigator."

"Then maybe *you* would like to talk to Mike and take his statement. Because there might be some other people that *you* should arrest."

"I already did," Steve said, turning up the volume on the TV.

"That was probably months ago. In the meantime, he and his brother are being threatened."

"He didn't have much to say then. Since he's concerned about repercussions at the job, I'm sure nothing's changed."

"But—"

"If no one's willing to name names... Sorry, but there's not a lot I can do."

Sick of hearing that answer, I folded my arms tight across my chest and glared at the former Seattle Mariner outfielder coming up to bat.

Steve settled back next to me. "Watch this guy strike out."

Having just struck out myself, I didn't find that prospect the least bit entertaining and reached for my phone.

That's when I noticed that I had a voice message from Gram. "Weird." I hadn't heard the phone ring.

"What?"

"I missed a call. Probably because it came in around the same time that you got here."

"I can be very distracting," he said, his breath warm on my ear.

I elbowed him in the ribs. "Now needs to not be one of those times." Because I was trying to listen to my grandmother's message.

"I just got off the phone with your mother. She's looking forward to your call. *Tonight*. Bye, sweetie," Gram said with a devious lilt in her voice.

I stared at my phone with disbelief. "Seriously?"

"Something wrong?" Steve asked.

"Yeah." I had just been set up.

Chapter Twenty-One

"Early lunch?" Patsy asked as I approached, casting a critical eye at the glass-domed anniversary clock next to her computer monitor. "Or are you off to pick up extra copies of the paper now that you're *famous*."

Patsy was the fourth person to mention the feature article in this morning's *Gazette* that I had been avoiding, and the last person I wanted to discuss it with.

I waved the certified letter in my hand like a hall pass. "Odette needs this mailed." Which gave me a good excuse to take a long lunch because I wanted to talk to Robin about that nine-one-one call before meeting my mother at her house at noon.

"I'll have some correspondence that you can take with you if you want to wait a few minutes."

Hang out with Patsy to give her an opportunity to dish out some snark about the car that *Mommy* bought me? No thanks. "This needs to go out right away." And so did I.

I spent my time waiting in line at the post office racking my brain for a plausible reason why Robin Kranick would be willing to talk to me about an incident that occurred over two years ago.

Fortunately, I had opted for a fairly professional image by wearing my black wool pantsuit. As a bonus I didn't have any stains on my blouse today, so when the curtains fluttered in response to the doorbell I'd rung twice, I was confident Robin would recognize that I wasn't there to sell her anything.

That didn't mean that she'd be any happier to see me, which became immediately apparent the second Robin cracked open the door.

"You're back," she stated with the same degree of warmth as in the hug Duke gives Marietta at Christmas.

"I am. Because of an official matter this time." I mentally kicked myself for my choice of words because I would surely lose my badge if this ever got back to Frankie.

The door opened wider, revealing Robin's autumn leaf-appliqué sweatshirt and a round face without a speck of makeup. "What official matter?"

"I wonder if we could talk inside," I said with a smile.

After a moment of hesitation she stepped back from the door. "Sure."

Sure? I wasn't expecting anything nearly so accommodating. But she knew me a little, so maybe I could get away with not making this too official of a matter.

Locking the door behind me, she set off down a narrow hallway. "Let me just turn off the stove."

I followed Robin and my nose into a huge kitchen tiled with mint green vinyl squares, where a saucepan was steaming on an ancient white stove surrounded by buttermilk Shaker cabinets. "Something smells good."

"I was making soup."

"I'll probably be having soup later myself," I said so that she wouldn't feel obligated to offer me any. "Now that it's getting colder outside, it's the perfect time of year for it."

Robin cracked an awkward smile as if she weren't accustomed to making small talk. "Let's go where it's more comfortable." She led me back through the entry way to a cozy living room with rose-patterned paper on two walls separated by painted bookshelves full of knickknacks.

Taking a seat next to the paperback romance on the blush velvet sofa, Robin picked up a remote to switch off the soap opera that had been blaring from the flat screen at the center of the bay window.

She flipped back the length of graying chestnut hair that had been encroaching on one of the leaves of her sweatshirt. "Okay, what's this matter that you need to speak with me about?"

I sat on the opposite end of the cushy sofa so that I could have a good view of her face. "As you and your brother have experienced over the last few weeks, there's always so much to do when someone passes away."

Knitting her brow, Robin gave me a confused look.

Since I was having trouble coming up with a non-official way of asking her about her mother's fall, I couldn't say that I blamed her. "That's also true for those of us in county government who have to process the paperwork."

"Why's the government involved in my mother's death?"

"All deaths produce paperwork. It's typically very routine. Cross the Ts, dot the Is. But sometimes we can't do our jobs without a little help from those who were closest to the deceased." I nodded as if my half-baked plea for her assistance made perfect sense. "And I can only imagine how close you were to your mom."

Robin's gaze tightened, her jaw muscles rigid with suspicion. "Uh-huh."

I pulled a notebook from my tote. "So would it be okay if I asked you a few questions?"

"I guess."

That had hardly been a ringing endorsement, but beggars couldn't be choosers. "Great."

"Would you say that your mom was accident-prone?"

Robin looked down at the round area rug that covered the majority of the dark hardwood between the coffee table and the TV. "Not especially."

"I understood that she took a pretty bad fall here a couple of years back."

Sucking in her lower lip, Robin nodded.

"Could you describe what happened?" I asked, watching the woman press her clasped hands tight to her chest as if she were praying.

"She tripped down the stairs and broke her clavicle."

"Where were you when this happened?"

"In my room."

The way Robin responded made it sound like she was guessing about what I'd be willing to believe—the tentative type of response that always sets off my "lie-dar."

"It was almost bedtime," she added, as if that might make the lie more credible.

"So you didn't see your mother fall?"

Her gaze fixed on that rug, Robin shook her head.

"What had been going on prior to her fall?"

"I don't understand."

"Like during dinner. I assume you had dinner together."

She nodded.

"Did it seem like your mom was in a fairly good mood?"

Robin didn't answer. Instead, it appeared as if a mental tug of war were playing out at the corners of her mouth.

"Okay, did anything happen around then that was out of the ordinary?"

"Maybe."

In other words, *yes*. "What was different about that evening?"

"Not a lot. We were just talking."

"About what?"

"You know, bills and stuff."

I had a feeling there was something pretty big packed into that *stuff*. "And how long after that would you say that your mom took that fall?"

"I don't know. Maybe an hour."

"Did she drink any wine that night?"

"Maybe." Robin shot me an icy glance. "I don't remember."

Yeah, you do. "I ask because it might have made her a little unsteady on her feet."

"She wasn't drunk, if that's what you're suggesting."

"I'm not trying to suggest anything." Okay, I was if alcohol was as much of a contributing factor to Naomi's fall as it was to her death. "I'm just asking."

"Why? What's it got to do with her death?"

"If her judgment were impaired—"

"My mother was *not* a drunk!" Robin declared, bolting to her feet.

That felt like the most honest thing she said since I arrived. "I'm very sorry, but the way her body was found—"

"I don't care for your insinuation, and I'd like you to leave."

Robin marched past me with more speed than I would have credited the big woman. With no choice but to follow, I met her at the front door.

But I couldn't walk out without matching her honesty with some of my own. "It would be really helpful in the determination of the cause of death if we could piece together everything that led to your mother getting into that tub."

Robin swung the door open, tears glistening in her eyes. "Well, I wasn't there, so there's not much I can tell you."

Dang, I believed her.

But while she might not bear any responsibility for her mother's drowning, it sure felt like Robin had every-thing to do with her mom moving into that condo in the first place.

After I stepped off the front porch and started down the walkway, it also felt like I was being watched. And for good reason, I realized when I spotted someone in an aqua blue jacket hiding behind the trunk of a pine tree in the next-door neighbor's yard.

I recognized the bird's nest of silver braids coiled on the top of Vivian Walker's head and gave her a friendly wave. "You know I can see you," I said under my breath.

I'd been acquainted with the seventy-something Duke's pie happy hour regular for a couple of decades, so I didn't hesitate when Mrs. Walker motioned me over.

But I did find it curious when she scurried across her lawn like an aging ninja to meet me in front of her open garage.

"How are you doing, Mrs. Walker?" *And what the heck are you up to?*

She snuck a peek at the Easley house as if to make sure Robin couldn't see us. "Any new developments?"

Huh? "What do you mean?"

Mrs. Walker squinted at me through oversized pink-framed glasses. "Well, since you're here, I assume the county has become involved."

Craparoonie. I didn't need any additional witnesses to the unauthorized death investigation I had been conducting.

My mouth went dry. "I—"

"That's what I read in this morning's paper, right? That you work for the assessor's office or something?"

Close enough. "Yes, but—"

"So the rumor's true."

I had no idea what she was talking about.

"They're behind in their taxes." A scowl accentuated the puckers surrounding Mrs. Walker's fuchsia-painted lips. "Of course, I knew Naomi was having money problems, especially after she decided to not sell the house."

"Was that something she talked to you about?"

The tiny woman cocked her head as she looked up at me. "Of course. I was probably her best friend."

Really. "Let's get out of this wind." It wasn't that brisk of a breeze whipping wisps of hair in front of my face. But the swirling undercurrents of potentially juicy gossip demanded more privacy, so I stepped into Mrs. Walker's garage with the hope that she'd follow.

"Good idea," she said, clearly no more eager to be observed by Robin than I was.

"What you said about Mrs. Easley deciding to keep the house—when was this?"

Vivian Walker folded her arms as she leaned against her faded red sedan. "A little over two years ago, right after the accident." She shook her head. "I really don't know how Naomi managed for as long as she did."

I'd seen how her bank balance was shrinking and didn't get it either.

"The scuttlebutt at Duke's," I said, lowering my voice as if this were fresh dirt from Gossip Central, "was that it had something to do with an arrangement that she made with Robin."

"Naomi let that girl get away with murder."

Maybe not literally.

"Don't get me wrong. I realize that what happened to Robin wasn't her fault. She was downright brutalized by that man."

I assumed that Mrs. Walker was referring to Hailey's father.

"Why, the things Naomi would tell me...just horrible. So it didn't surprise me in the least when she and Earl took the girls in. It was only right. But twenty years later, when it was just the two of them in the house... If you ask me, Robin had her mother wrapped around her little finger." Mrs. Walker held her arms tight as if she needed the warmth. "So yes, I guess you could say an arrangement was reached. Although that's not the word I would have used."

"Because Mrs. Easley didn't want to stress out her daughter with a move?"

Vivian Walker hooted as if I'd told her a groaner of a joke. "Because she didn't want to get thrown down the stairs again."

Holy cannoli. "That's how that accident happened?"

"They had 'words.' That's all Naomi would tell me. But I can put two and two together."

Which fit with what little Robin had revealed to me about that night.

Mrs. Walker's pink lips curled into a calculating smile as she locked on my gaze. "And since the county is now getting involved, I can only assume that this 'arrangement' might finally be coming to an end."

"That's not for me to say." Truly.

"Well, something needs to happen pretty soon. Just

look at that yard. It's become a real eyesore."

"If Robin decides to sell, she'll have to do something about all those weeds."

"Maybe," Mrs. Walker said with a twinkle in her eye. "You never know who might be interested in buying the place."

I didn't let on that I already knew about the offers that she and her neighbors had recently received from the Cascara development company.

She shrugged. "Of course, it's not just her decision, but I have a feeling that Gordon will be agreeable to the right offer."

And I had a feeling that Mrs. Walker's conversation with Gordon Easley had already happened.

Chapter Twenty-Two

"You're late," my mother announced as I stepped onto a gorgeous Persian rug that I couldn't remember having seen before.

"Sorry. I had to drop something off at the post office for work." It wasn't to my advantage to mention the other stops I made along the way.

I pointed at the luxurious rug spanning the hardwood between the door and the curved staircase like an indoor flower garden. "Is this new?"

Heaving a weary sigh, Marietta glided past me in bare feet. "I had it in Santa Monica."

"Okay." I had spent most of my summers there as a child. I didn't remember any Persian rugs. It didn't matter. I hadn't come here to talk about her furnishings.

"Would you like some coffee?" she asked while I trailed in her musky jasmine wake.

My mother didn't know how to make a decent cup of coffee. "No thanks."

She pulled up the cover of an appliance garage and plucked out a coffee pod from a three-tier storage rack.

"I have your favorite. Italian roast—what you served Barry and me when we got back from our honeymoon, right?"

Shocked that she remembered, I nodded.

Satisfaction tugged at the edges of her Cupid's bow mouth as she loaded the pod into her coffeemaker. "Yes, my darling. I've been paying attention."

Sometimes. "Is that a new coffeemaker?"

"Cute, isn't it?" Marietta stroked the humming machine as if it were a cat waking up from a long nap in that cozy compartment. "Barry bought it for me as a homecoming present."

Probably because he hated her coffee as much as I did.

"Nice." Even nicer, I didn't see any other new acquisitions as I looked around, so maybe my mother was finally satisfied with her new life in Port Merritt.

And maybe I could reach some level of acceptance with my thunder thighs.

It would never happen, but it didn't prevent me from clinging to the hope.

I noticed that the glass table in the breakfast nook overlooking a back deck large enough for a square dance had been set for two with her good china. But I didn't smell anything cooking or see any trace of food preparation in her immaculate kitchen.

"Pretty," I said, aware of Marietta watching my every movement like a hungry bird of prey.

"I wasn't sure what you'd like for lunch. I have salad, but I could also scramble a couple of eggs if you prefer."

"Salad's fine." We both knew that tossing vegetables into a bowl pushed the limits of her culinary abilities.

"Okay. Have a seat."

Seconds later, she placed a bowl of Cobb salad in front of me that looked identical to the premade salad I had picked up for Rox and me two days earlier.

Which was just fine. Sharing a meal was awkward enough. At least now I didn't have to worry about her giving me food poisoning.

"This looks good," I said as she took the seat adjacent to me.

Marietta flashed me a cautious smile. "I'm glad you're here."

"Me too." Sort of.

After a moment of companionable crunching, I had the feeling that we had just exchanged the Digby girl equivalent of apologies.

With her fork poised over her bowl, my mother slanted me a glance. "Everything okay?"

"Everything's great."

Her extended lashes fluttered over her cheeks like butterflies dancing a jig.

Yep. That was as close as her mouth could come to uttering an "I'm sorry."

"Did you happen to see the article in the paper?" Marietta asked between dainty sips of coffee almost ten minutes later.

I kept my eyes focused on the bacon bits at the bottom of my bowl. "Not yet." And I intended to keep it that way. "Are you happy with how it turned out?"

"Oh, yes. The picture of the two of us that Renee used is especially good. I'm going to ask her to send it to me so that I can have it framed."

Whatever.

"Also, about that," my mother started to say when her doorbell rang.

Pushing away from the table, she squinted at the antique pendulum wall clock hanging in the family room. "Can't anyone be on time today?"

Since half of that remark was aimed at me, I bit back a sigh. "Who is it?"

"If it's my contractor," she said, the soles of her feet slapping the hardwood, "he's very early."

While my mother modulated her voice into Southern fried Marietta Moreau mode at the door, I cleared the table and took the next few minutes to wash the dishes.

Whatever purpose was behind this appointment with her contractor, by the volume of honey that Marietta kept injecting into every sentence, I could only assume that she wanted something the guy wasn't too keen on providing.

One thing was for sure: I didn't have a part to play in this particular act. But I also couldn't leave before she and I talked about the other reason for my visit: the car. So I followed their voices past the curved staircase to the great room, where I found a man in a navy jacket running his palm over a low section of sage green wall.

"We can easily fix this," he said as I waited to get my mother's attention. "I apologize. I don't know why this wasn't done right the first time."

At least someone in this house could issue a proper apology.

"Oh, Charmaine." Marietta waved me over. "Come in and meet Gary Carpp—"

Did she say Carpp?

"—the man who built this beautiful house."

"Not by myself, I didn't," the man in his late forties said, extending his hand as I approached.

He seemed friendly enough and had a solid hand-shake. There was no reason for the hair at the back of my neck to stand on end other than the fact that his jacket was emblazoned with a Cascara Construction Group logo. And even then, I had no reason to suspect that he had anything to do with the intimidation tactics the Pollard brothers had been experiencing.

"Charmaine Digby. And I'm sorry, I don't know that I heard your name correctly."

A disarming smile split his face. "If I had a nickel for every time someone said that, I could have retired by now. Gary Carpp, like the fish."

"Any relation to Dr. Carpp, the dentist?"

"My older brother. I'm the better-looking one. And you didn't need to introduce yourself, Charmaine. I recognized you from your picture in this morning's paper."

Swell.

His cell phone rang and he pulled it from the pocket of his blue jeans without masking his irritation. "Sorry, ladies. Looks like duty calls back at the office."

After disconnecting, he assured my mother that his scheduler would be giving her a call, and they exchanged good-byes at the door.

"Lovely man," Marietta said after she clicked the door shut. "I far prefer dealing with him than the underling they sent the first time. That guy hardly gave me the time of day."

I stood at the window and experienced another prickly feeling while I watched Gary climb into the white van parked in the driveway. "He obviously didn't know who you are." Or didn't care.

Marietta heaved a sigh. "You make it sound like I expect the star treatment all the time."

"Sorry. I just meant..." There was no way out of the hole I was digging, so it was best to toss aside the shovel. "Who exactly is Gary in the Cascara Construction food chain?"

"One of the owners. Or maybe he's the son of the owner." My mother padded toward the kitchen. "Whatever his position, he's high enough on the ladder to suit me."

"Thank goodness for that," I muttered under my breath as Gary eased the van past Gram's SUV parked out front. And then my heart hammered out an alarm when I got an eyeful of the company logo on the passenger side door. "Holy crap! That's a tree on his van."

"What did you think Cascara stood for, silly? Even I know it's a tree."

"But it's a tree on a white van." And his brother is a dentist.

Holy crap!

✳

"Honey, you don't really think that Gary Carpp had anything to do with Naomi Easley's drowning," Donna said while we waited for her six o'clock appointment to show up at the salon.

Too restless to sit still, I spun around in her black and chrome styling chair as I tried to piece together everything I thought I knew to be true about what happened the day of Mrs. Easley's death. "If I had told you that I saw a guy with some sort of company van visit my neighbor a couple of hours before she was found dead, wouldn't you find that at least a little bit suspicious?"

"Sure, but—"

"And if I swore he'd been there with my dentist, wouldn't that make you wonder what that was all about?"

Donna tucked the broom she had been using to tidy up between appointments into the closet next to the shampoo bowl. "Yes. But as far as I know, your memory is still pretty reliable."

"Come on," I said, dragging the toe of my black pump to stop the spinning. "Althea identified the van, a tree guy, and her dentist. And Mavis saw them too. She was just so focused on her sister at the time that she didn't get a good look at them."

"Even if they were there that day," Donna said with a dismissive wave of her hand. "And I think it's highly unlikely. It doesn't mean that Gary and his brother did anything wrong."

"Maybe not intentionally." Because Naomi Easley still ended up dead.

"Really? You spend one minute with the guy and then see a tree on his van, and you're ready to make a citizen's arrest?"

"Don't be ridiculous." If I had any real proof, I wouldn't dream of making a citizen's arrest; I'd call Steve to do it.

"Because I know the man, and I'm telling you there's no way that he'd hurt a nice, little old lady."

"You cut his hair?"

Donna nodded. "And you should see how sweet he is to all the girls when he comes in. As charming as can be."

"I bet." Because something behind all that charm had made my hair stand on end.

"Well, hon, if I can't convince you, you'll just have to put him to your lie detector test and come to your own conclusions."

"Yeah, sure." I didn't know when I'd have the opportunity to do that with the younger of the two Carpp brothers, but I might have one tomorrow at my dentist appointment. Because he and his brother might have been two of the last people to see Naomi Easley before she died.

"Oh, hey! I almost forgot." Donna grabbed a folded newspaper from the magazine rack behind her three-chair waiting area, turned to the back page, and dropped it in my lap. "Nice picture."

Groaning, I refolded the paper and handed it back to her. "Don't remind me."

"What's the matter? It's a great shot."

"Well, the story that went along with it wasn't so great, was it?"

Donna gave me a blank stare. "Was there something about it that upset Mr. Ferris? Because—"

"Mr. Ferris! Didn't you see the part about how Marietta showed she was so different from the terrible mother she played?"

"Huh?"

Why was Donna being so dense? "That's the real story behind the car she bought me."

"Your mom bought you a car?"

"That's why Renee shot that picture of the two of us. I was supposed to look the part of the grateful recipient."

"When did your mom buy you a car?"

Good grief, Donna! "It's in that story. Didn't you read it?"

She shook her head. "Delle Lundgren read it to me while I touched up her roots. The only place you're mentioned is that picture. Although there might have been a line or two about where you and Mr. Ferris work."

I snatched the paper away from her and scanned the article.

Marietta Moreau, the former Mary Jo Digby, born and raised in Port Merritt... Co-starring role in the new release, *Loving Lucian*, blah, blah, blah. Recently married to Port Merritt High School biology teacher Barry Ferris, blah, blah, blah. Enjoying married life back home, blah, blah, blah.

I looked into Donna's sapphire almond eyes. "I'm

barely mentioned."

"That's what I told you."

"I don't understand. My mother engineered that interview to slant it a very specific way," I said. Then my cell phone started ringing.

"It seemed pretty positive to me. Isn't she happy with it?"

"She said she was."

"Then what's the problem?"

"What the heck am I supposed to do about the car?"

I reached down to grab my phone from my tote and saw that my grandmother was calling. "Hi, Gram."

"Wait a minute!" Donna planted her fists on her hips. "What car?"

I waved Donna away to shush her. "I'm sorry, Gram, what?"

"I said, are you going to be here soon?" she asked. "Stevie's here and—"

"I am *so* sorry. I'm on my way." Disconnecting, I grabbed my tote and headed for the door. "Gotta go. I'm late for dinner." Again.

"Char, wait!" Donna followed me out the door. "You haven't told me. What car?!"

Chapter Twenty-Three

"You're late," Steve announced, greeting me at my grandmother's back door.

"I'm well aware." I gave him a quick kiss and then turned to the lady with the peachy cotton-candy hair waiting expectantly. "I am so sorry. I was with Donna and lost track of time."

Gram shooed me out of her kitchen. "Go wash up. Dinner's ready."

In other words, don't be late next time.

Five minutes later, I felt her eyes on me while I ladled gravy into the crater of mashed potatoes on my plate. "What? Am I hogging the gravy?"

"Yes," Steve answered for her as he pulled the gravy boat in front of his heaping plate.

Gram shook her head as if she wanted to give us a lecture on table manners. "No, I was just wondering how your day went."

I had no desire to put myself in the middle of a firing squad of criticism with these two at the table. "Fine."

Looking down, she sliced off a tiny bite of roast beef,

which appeared to be an avoidance maneuver, but failed miserably to disguise the pleasure lighting her eyes. "Did you happen to see your mother?"

I stabbed a limp broccoli spear and pointed it at her. "You know I did."

She shrugged. "Well, I may have heard a little something about you two having lunch."

"Then you already know how the play date you set up went."

"You two had a play date?" Steve chimed in as he reached for another biscuit. "How cute."

I aimed my best withering stare at him. "Don't make this more uncomfortable than it already is."

Gram set down her fork. "But I thought it went really well."

"It went well enough." And I hoped to leave it at that.

She narrowed her eyes at me while I chewed on the broccoli spear that she had overcooked. "That's it?"

What did she want? "We didn't exactly hug it out, if that's what you were expecting."

"But your mother called Renee to make sure that she took out any mention of the car. Surely, that deserves a little more—"

"I didn't know that at the time."

Gram leaned in. "What do you mean, you didn't know? It was obvious from that feature in this morning's paper."

Buckling under the weight of her disappointment in me, I studied the gravy congealing on my plate. "Since I'd had a preview of what Renee was going to write, I wasn't especially interested in reading it."

"And I suppose your mother never mentioned it."

I shook my head. "If she intended to, we got interrupted."

Gram split the biscuit on her plate and buttered it. "You do realize that was her way of apologizing."

I realized that on my way over from Donatello's. "Yep."

"So what's gonna happen with the car?" Steve asked, his mouth half full.

I gaped at him. "You are really not helping tonight."

He shot me an innocent smile. "I was just asking."

"Certainly, you discussed it when you were over there," Gram said.

I knew she wouldn't give me any credit for good intentions, and I couldn't very well mention the tree guy who cut my lunch date short in front of Steve. "Why don't we talk about this later?"

She dropped the biscuit she had been nibbling on. "Charmaine! Do you mean to tell me that you two didn't get anything settled about that car?"

"We ran out of time because I had to get back to work," I said, hating how lame that sounded.

"These biscuits are great, Eleanor. I shouldn't..." Steve reached past me for another one. "But I will. Want to pass me the butter there, Chow Mein?"

He pressed his shoulder into mine when I handed him the butter dish, his breath warm on my ear. "Who says I'm not a help?"

Since the temperature level of the scorn emanating

from the head of the table remained high enough to fry my potatoes, I patted Steve's knee. "Nice try."

"So?" Gram demanded.

"Like I said, we ran out of—"

She raised her hand to cut me off. "Honesty this time, please."

"Mom's contractor arrived during lunch and pretty much got us sidetracked." Which was certainly the truth as far as I was concerned. "And then I really did have to get back to the office."

Gram aimed an icy stare at me. "Then you'll have to go back tomorrow."

"I might have plans tomorrow." Which, depending on what my new dentist had to tell me, might very well be the case.

"And I'm getting tired of seeing that car parked out front that no one is doing anything about, so I suggest that you rearrange your schedule so that you can talk this out once and for all with your mother."

I stifled a cringe. "Fine."

Gram wagged an arthritic finger at my plate. "Now eat your food. It's getting cold."

I'd lost my appetite.

After we finished the dishes and left my grandmother napping in her recliner, I walked Steve home across the street.

His arm curled around my waist as we stepped onto his front porch. "I hope you have something else in mind beyond seeing me safely home." As he angled to kiss me, Steve's eyes glinted dark as sin.

"I do," I said, delighting in his touch. "Open the door."

"Yes, ma'am." He unlocked his door and pulled me inside.

Just as Steve pressed me against the wall and started lavishing my neck with kisses, I gently pushed him away. "I'd like to talk to you."

Looking down at me, his brow furrowed. "Talk?"

"For a few minutes. Consider it foreplay."

"I seriously doubt that what you have to say is going to resemble foreplay."

I pointed at his cocoa brown leather sectional. "Sit."

Steve took a seat and folded his arms. "This had better not be what I think it's about."

I shushed him. "I just need your opinion about something."

"Okay."

"Remember what I said about my mother's contractor arriving when I was there today?"

He sharpened his gaze. "What about it?"

"It was Gary Carpp, some muckety-muck with the company that built her house. I guess there's been an ongoing issue with some cracks that need to be fixed."

Steve shrugged a shoulder. "Okay."

"Do you know him?"

"Yeah."

"From some interactions with him?" Like an arrest?

"If you want to call a county council meeting an interaction. But I mainly know him from coaching one of his kids a couple of years back."

"That's it?" I asked, inching closer to study his face.

He smirked. "You can look as long as you'd like. I got nothing else for you."

"Really? That's all you've got?"

"What exactly were you hoping for?"

"I don't know. There's just something about him that's a little creepy." And that was before I realized that he was the *tree guy*.

Steve extended his arm in invitation, and I nestled next to him on the sectional. "Is your mother concerned about having this guy in her house or something?"

"No. I think I was the only one of the two of us who thought something felt a little off."

"Probably because you were looking for trouble."

"At my mother's?" I rested my head on his shoulder. "Hardly."

"Chow Mein, you're always looking for trouble." Steve leaned back and pulled me on top of him. "And I do believe you just found some."

Chapter Twenty-Four

After I completed all the paperwork for my seven-thirty appointment with Dr. Carpp, I figured that I might as well take advantage of the empty waiting room and see what I could find out from Tessa, his receptionist.

I was acquainted with Tessa from having gone to high school with her husband, Colby. So after we got caught up with how she and Colby had adjusted to life with twin girls, I mentioned how I had been with Rox when I cracked my filling.

"Roxanne was quick to recommend Dr. Carpp," I said, leaning on the white counter separating us.

Tessa smiled. "We always appreciate patient recommendations."

"Oh, she wasn't the only one. Robin Kranick also told me to come here." Or might have if the subject had ever come up.

"Robin Kranick?" Tessa offered up a blank look. "That name doesn't sound familiar."

"Really? She made it sound like her mother had been a longtime patient. I'm sure you remember her. Naomi

Easley?"

"Oh, I remember Naomi. She and her husband came to my wedding. But she was never a patient." Tessa chuckled. "Not that we mind people patronizing the competition. If they didn't, this waiting room would be standing room only."

Okay. It was good to know that the "house call" that Althea witnessed didn't take place because of some doctor/patient relationship.

"Still, it was really helpful to hear such glowing reviews. It's been a while since I've had a checkup, so I'm a little nervous about it." Especially since Althea's dentist and his brother the "tree guy" were two of the last people to see Naomi alive.

"Charmaine, you're gonna love how gentle Greg is. Everyone does."

Tessa's biased endorsement didn't make me any less nervous, and by the time Samantha, the dental assistant, fastened a baby blue paper bib under my chin, my heart was thumping like a kettledrum.

"Relax," she said, patting my arm after she finished taking a set of X rays. "The doctor will only be doing an exam today, so you'll hardly feel a thing."

Since Naomi had probably been so out of it that she didn't feel much the night she drowned, I didn't find that very reassuring.

"Breathe," I told myself, trying to slow my pulse while I stared at a watercolor in blues and greens. No doubt the tranquil seascape had been chosen to give the patient something calming to focus on in an otherwise austere environment.

This patient's pulse, however, refused to be calmed and hammered in my ear as if I'd been swimming laps in that seascape. Unfortunately, despite the cool air circulating the office, I was also sweating so I blotted my face with my paper bib.

That's when a taller, grayer version of Gary Carpp in a white lab coat walked up next to my chair.

"Charmaine?" he asked, offering a bright smile while he extended his hand.

Crap.

"Hi." I smoothed the bib over my chest and shook his hand.

"Greg Carpp. I understand you've got a sensitive tooth."

"I bit down on something hard and it hasn't been the same since."

"I like to think of that as nature's way of reminding people that they should make an appointment to see their dentist." He winked. "But I'm pretty sure it doesn't work that way."

I forced a smile and gave my upper lip another swipe when he turned to look at the computer monitor at the desk to my right.

"I see it's been a couple of years since your last checkup," Dr. Carpp said.

"You know how it is when you move and have to find new doctors."

He nodded at my feeble response while flipping the screen to study my X rays.

I needed to say something to grab his attention. "Fortunately, I was visiting Althea Flanders and she was telling me about you. Actually, you and your brother."

Dr. Carpp turned, focusing on me over the wire-frame reading glasses he had put on. "What's this now?"

"I guess you and your brother were visiting the lady who lived across the street, Naomi Easley," I said, watching him carefully for a reaction.

The pleasant expression slipped from his face like butter off a stack of pancakes. "Hunh."

"You made an impression." And the one you're making right now tells me you're not happy about it.

"Naomi was a nice lady. It's a shame what happened."

He didn't look that broken up about it to me. "A real shame."

Seemingly eager to change the subject, Dr. Carpp swiveled over in his chair while Samantha blinded me with the overhead light. "Let's take a look and see what's going on, shall we?" he said, adjusting the dental chair back so quickly that it felt like a warning about who here would be making that discovery.

While I knew I was in no serious danger as long as I could see Samantha standing over my left shoulder, that didn't prevent fresh beads of sweat from oozing from my every pore.

Within seconds, Samantha reached behind her to direct a portable fan at me, and then whispered in my ear, "I get hot flashes too."

Even though she had just aged me a few years, I appreciated having an ally in the room, especially while one of my prime suspects was pointing a sharp instrument at me.

"Relax and open wide," he told me.

Relax. Sure. That could happen.

I sunk my nails into the vinyl armrests. *Please don't hurt me.*

I spent the next few minutes trying to remember to breathe while the man poked around in my mouth. By the time Samantha freed me from the confines of my blue bib, the only pain I felt was when Dr. Carpp informed me that I'd need to come back to have not just the one cracked filling replaced, but I needed a new filling to address the cavity that had developed on the tooth next to it.

"How much will that cost?" I asked Tessa after I made my way back to the front desk.

"With your insurance plan, probably a little over a hundred dollars." She brightened. "We have an opening tomorrow afternoon if you'd like to get this taken care of."

With a looming car repair bill poised to wipe out my savings, I had no desire to go further in the red. "I can live with this for a little while." Plus, until I ruled out the Carpp brothers as suspects, I didn't want to give one of them permission to come at me with a drill. "After I check my calendar, I'll call to schedule an appointment." Maybe.

"No problem." Tessa propped her elbows on her desk. "So, what'd you think of Greg?"

I thought he was hiding something.

Did that make him a murderer? No.

But there was something about how his demeanor changed when I mentioned Naomi's name that gave me the willies.

"You were right. He was very gentle." With me, anyway.

After confirming with Georgie that he'd have my car ready for me when I got off work, I caught up with the filing, and then settled in at my desk for the rest of the morning to run background checks for one of the paralegals in the criminal division.

As long as I was searching for criminal history, I typed in Greg and Gary Carpp's names. Neither brother had much of a checkered past. Gary, a resident of Port Townsend, had a misdemeanor battery charge that got dropped after the guy he punched failed to appear, and some traffic citations from over twenty years ago, while Greg the dentist received a speeding ticket from the state patrol last year.

Big deal.

The much more interesting information came from the Cascara Development Group website. There, while boasting about the luxurious homes they had constructed in the greater Seattle area, the privately held parent of Cascara Construction portrayed itself as being family oriented by featuring the ownership group on a biography page.

I zoomed in on a picture that the caption identified as

company founder and president John Carpp alongside his wife, Margaret, and smiling sons Gary and Greg back when they were in their twenties.

While the image conveyed home and hearth, it also projected the spirit behind the heading at the top of the page: *Let our family build your family's dream home.*

"Is that why you were there with your brother, Greg?" I asked the future dentist staring back at me. As a representative of your family's business?

It was the only thing that made sense. Especially since their visit to Naomi Easley's condo fit in the same timeframe as when Byron's family was approached.

That didn't mean they would have had motivation to harm Mrs. Easley if they failed to persuade her to sell her house. Then again, if she had been the lone holdout on that block, millions of dollars of potential profit could be very motivating.

Chapter Twenty-Five

"Charmaine Digby to see Mrs. Ferris," I told the same uniformed security guard who had stopped me in front of Marietta's gated community yesterday.

The middle-aged man with the beer belly hanging over his belt gave me a long look before thumbing through the pages on his clipboard. "You're not on the list."

Give me a big break. "You remember me from around this time yesterday, right?"

He nodded politely. "Yes, ma'am."

"And I was on the list then, right?"

"You sure were."

"Okay, then will you buzz me in, please?"

"Sorry, you're not on today's list."

Did this guy think he was guarding Fort Knox or something? "Then please call Mrs. Ferris so that she can tell you it's okay to let her daughter in."

"I really am sorry, but I'm not allowed to call her before noon."

Fortunately, I didn't have to abide by Marietta's "Do

not disturb" notices. "Give me a minute," I told him while I called her cell phone number.

"Charmaine," she said, picking up after one ring. "What a nice surprise."

"Didn't Gram tell you I was coming over?"

"Uh, she may have mentioned it."

"Well, I'm at the front gate and ..." I squinted at the name embroidered on the security guard's khaki shirt. "You failed to pass that information along to Hank so I'm not on the *list*."

Marietta uttered a less than genteel curse word. "May I speak with him, please?"

I handed Hank my phone, heard him offer his assurances that this inconvenience wouldn't happen again, and then he said much the same thing when he handed me back my phone.

But I wasn't as interested in being elevated to VIP status as I was in locating the current Cascara Construction job site. So after I hung up with Marietta, I asked for directions.

Hank promptly scurried over to his guard shack to open the wrought iron gate and returned with a visitor's map. "Thinking of buying?" he asked after circling the tract of approximately twenty hillside homes at the outer rim of the subdivision that would complete construction at Bayview Estates.

And live even closer to my mother? I forced a smile. "Just taking a gander at the location for my neighbor."

Giving him a wave, I eased through the open gate before it closed on me, and then snaked past two dozen million-dollar homes until I reached the highest point on the bluff, where I spotted a construction trailer on wheels.

I slowed, checking out the vehicles parked in front of two of the houses being framed. The beater van parked behind a faded blue pickup didn't have any trees on the side panels, and the other four cars were not new enough to double as company vehicles, so I pulled up in front of the construction trailer and climbed out of Gram's SUV.

Since I had been short on time this morning, I hadn't done much with my hair or makeup, and my yoga pants and pink cotton tunic probably made me look like I had taken a wrong turn for an exercise class. But with several heads swiveling as I stepped on a wooden plank that provided a path across one of the muddy lots, I hoped that might work to my advantage.

"Is Mike here?" I asked the scruffy twenty-year-old with the hammer looking down at me from a ladder.

"Mike," he shouted. "You got company."

Within seconds, Mike Pollard glowered at me from the second story. "What do you want?"

I shielded my eyes from the glare reflecting off of the puffy white cloud above him. "A minute of your time."

When a guy who looked like a young version of Gary Carpp appeared over his shoulder, Mike pointed at the aluminum trailer behind me. "Over there."

Going back the way I had come, I waited by the steps of the trailer as instructed and watched two men pounding nails up on the second story. Neither resembled a

Carpp.

I didn't see any other movement up there, but I wouldn't be able to tell if there was anyone working at the rear of the house without crossing the street for a better vantage point. And with the scowl hanging from Mike's brow as he climbed down a ladder, I knew this was not the time to do anything besides plant my feet.

I pasted what I hoped was a pleasant smile on my face while Mike glided across the wooden plank with surprising grace for a big man. But there was nothing the least bit graceful with how he stomped past me up the steps without an acknowledgment of my presence.

"Come on," he said, holding the door of the trailer open for me.

I felt tremors as if the earth were shifting under my feet as I stepped around a metal desk layered with building plans. "Sorry to pull you away from your work."

Mike closed the door and took a seat at the desk. "Never mind that. What are you here for?"

I inched closer so that I could see him better in the dim light that four little windows provided the cramped workspace. "I wanted to ask if you've had any trouble from Gary or Greg Carpp."

Mike gave me a long look. "Trouble like what?"

"Like anything beyond ordinary work stuff."

"I wouldn't call it trouble."

I needed him to keep talking. "What exactly?"

"Gary can be a hothead. You find out fast to stay on his good side."

"Or what?"

"He can get in your face."

"Like confrontational?"

Removing his ball cap, Mike raked his fingers through his short, dark hair. "I guess."

"Have you ever heard about him getting physical with anyone?" I asked, thinking about the battery charge that had earned Gary a court date.

Mike's mouth formed a straight line while he stared at his well-worn running shoes. "Nope."

That looked more like a *yes* to me. "Okay. Have you ever heard Gary threaten anybody?

"If this is about Ryan—"

"It's not. Not directly, anyway." I inched a little closer. "How about it? Did Gary ever make it sound like he was going to hurt someone?"

Giving me a smirk of contempt, Mike pushed out of the chair. "I need to get back to work, and you need to leave."

I clasped his forearm, touching solid muscle. "What about Greg?"

"I don't deal with him. Gary's the only one I have to answer to." Mike opened the door. "And I'd like to keep my job."

I turned to him after he followed me down the steps. "Mike, I have a friend who might be getting pressured to sell to these guys." It was a little late to use Naomi Easley this way, but with this mountain of a man ready to kick me off his job site, it was the only play I had left. "Should she be concerned about what they might do?"

He shot me a dismissive glance. "They care too much

about their professional reputation."

Okay, then I needed to stop imagining a Carpp brother pushing Naomi Easley's head below the surface of that water.

"At least I used to think they cared," he muttered as he walked away.

Dang. Mike might as well have lit a match under my imagination.

"Where have you been?" my mother asked, waiting for me at her front door wearing a tiger-striped tunic and black yoga pants like mine, only two sizes smaller. And I was pretty sure that she hadn't found hers at Valu-Mart.

I gave her a quick hug. "I stopped to talk to a guy I met a couple of days ago."

Her glossy lips curled into a knowing smile. "Does Steve have some competition in the neighborhood?"

"No, nothing like that. This guy's just someone I met through work." But I wasn't here to talk about the men in my life.

"I have to be back at the office in a half hour, so I need to make this fast," I said, heading to the table where we had lunch yesterday.

"Have you eaten?" Marietta opened her refrigerator. "I have some leftover sesame chicken from last night. And I didn't make it. Barry did, so you know it will be edible."

"No, I don't have time." I pushed out the chair next to me. "Mom, please sit."

She fixed her gaze on the chair as if I had attached an electric current to it and then pulled up the cover of her appliance garage. "Sounds like this is a conversation that calls for coffee."

And that sounded like a stall tactic. "Really, I don't have time."

Heaving a sigh, Marietta slammed the cover shut. "Iced tea, then. It's already made."

"Fine!" Whatever it took to get her undivided attention.

"Oh, I meant to tell you yesterday," Marietta said seconds later when she placed two ice-filled tumblers on the table. "Guess who I've seen making the rounds on the morning shows."

I didn't need to guess. I'd seen him myself. "I know. Chris has been out there, pushing his cookbook."

Settling her enviably tight tush in the seat next to me, she flicked a gold-bangled wrist as if she were shooing away a fly. "He's a jerk of the first order, but I'd kill to have his publicist. The man is everywhere."

"He certainly is." My ex was also the last person I wanted to talk about today. "I—"

"How are you doing with his other news?"

Marietta rested her soft palm on my left hand and gazed into my eyes so tenderly I had to reach for my tea to cool the burn of threatening tears.

"It doesn't matter," I said, trying to bury my lie between sips, and then the icy sweet tea washed over my cracked filling and I about jumped out of my skin.

My mother sat at the edge of her seat, her face inches

from mine as I pressed my hand to my jaw. "What's wrong?"

"Nothing."

"I don't wish to call my daughter a liar, but it looks to me like you have a sore tooth."

I pushed the glass of tea away. "It will be okay in a second."

With a smirk of skepticism tugging at the corner of her mouth, she cupped my chin to inspect every inch of my face. "I don't think so."

I felt like we were dancing at the edge of a giant rabbit hole, but I had no intention of jumping in with her. "Mom, really—"

"You're blocked."

"Excuse me?"

"Your *chi*, it's blocked."

I leaned back to get out of her reach. "My *chi* is fine and dandy, and has nothing to do with me biting down on a nutshell and cracking a filling."

"Oh, my dear. Trust me." She spread her tapered fingers in front of my face like a magician. "Your blockage is almost palpable."

"Says you." And no one else I knew.

"It's feeding that negativity, so no wonder you're in pain."

"Uh-huh."

"And now I understand why."

For a woman who had only recently made an attempt to become a part of my life, Marietta hadn't earned the right to pretend that she understood what made me tick.

"Let's not—"

"It's Chris swirling around in there," she said, pointing at my chest.

Okay, this ridiculous dance was over. "It's not. I—"

"I should have seen it before. Why you hesitated to take the house."

Because I didn't want her as my landlord.

"Why the only relationship you seem to be willing to commit to is with a dog."

"I don't need you of all people judging my relationships."

She winced for a nanosecond as if I had landed a physical blow and then gave me the prettiest of fake smiles. "Maybe not. But my darling, as someone who has experienced the benefit of purging negative male energy from her life, let me give you some motherly advice."

Biting back the curse word at the tip of my tongue, I weighed my alternatives. Listen to Marietta's half-baked advice or suffer my grandmother's wrath because I bolted instead of having an honest conversation with my mother. "Fine. Just make it fast. I have to—"

"Get back to work." Marietta patted my hand. "I know. Sweetheart, I also know how much it hurt when Chris walked out on you."

Crossing my arms, I stared at the glass tabletop to distance myself from the compassion glinting in her eyes.

"You must realize that you open yourself up to his negative energy every time you get into his old car."

Good grief. "Really, Mom. It's just a car."

"It's not just a car. It's *his* car, full of his touch, his smell."

"I had it detailed. It doesn't have the stench of his cologne anymore."

"Maybe not, but you can't clean out his energy. Why it probably radiates from the seat every time you get behind the wheel."

Into my butt? That was a mental image that I needed to purge from my brain.

She flicked her wrist at me again. "No wonder it's always breaking down."

"Come on, it's just an old, temperamental car."

"Temperamental because he made it that way. Didn't you tell me that it broke down before you even made it out of California?"

I should never tell her anything.

"And it's in the shop *again*. It's like he cursed it because he couldn't stand losing it to you, and now you'll never be free of his curse until you're free of that car."

Her droning on about curses sounded way too much like she was quoting a line from one of her old horror movies. "I'm sure the Jag isn't cursed." It just acted that way periodically.

"Maybe not literally, but I'm telling you, my darling. It's time to free yourself from everything that's keeping the *chi* from flowing. You'll feel ever so much better."

Right. "If we're going to talk about me freeing myself of negative things, you're going to have to help me."

Marietta brightened. "Of course. Anything."

"You need to respect my privacy."

"But I do."

"Not when you make decisions for me, you don't."

"But—"

"So, no more cars, no more housing upgrades," I said, counting each item off with my finger. "No more exercise equipment, or furniture that you think I need. I say when I need something new—especially a car—not you."

She sniffed, her long lashes shuttering her glistening eyes. "I was only trying to help."

"Okay, we both know there's a lot more to that story. But you killed it before it got into the paper, and I appreciate that."

"I wasn't trying to use you as a *prop*, as you put it." Marietta swiped at a tear, creating a powdery makeup smear. "I just got a little carried away when Renee overheard that you needed a new car."

"She probably saw an angle she could work to her advantage."

"Probably. And when she mentioned that she could get me a good deal…" My mother snuck a glance at me. "Well, I do enjoy buying at a discount."

"I've noticed. But it seems like you've been acquiring a lot of things lately. It's not a competition, you know," I said, trying to inject a little levity into what was becoming an increasingly awkward conversation.

Her gaze sharpened. "I do believe that you should respect my privacy as well. Because how I choose to spend my money is my business."

"Absolutely. We just don't want you to…" How could I tell my mother that I wasn't the only one who had concerns about how much of her savings she had blown through since she moved back to town? "You know, until your house in California sells, maybe—"

"My financial situation is just fine, thank you very much."

I didn't believe that for a minute, but I had no desire to call Marietta on her bluff and piss her off more than she already was. Not when I required her cooperation to move that new car parked in front of Gram's.

"Great." Rising from the table, I grabbed my tote. "On that happy note, I've gotta go. But before I do, could I have the keys to the Subaru?"

My mother's eyes widened. "Didn't you just make it very clear that you don't want the car?"

"If I'm going to return it, I need the keys and all the paperwork."

With a little pout at her lips, Marietta disappeared into the office opposite the great room and met me in the entryway with a clear zippered envelope. "Everything should be in here."

"Thanks," I said, reaching for the envelope but she held on tight.

"Before you do anything, promise me that you'll think about freeing yourself of that man."

And his cursed car. *Yeah, yeah.* "I will. Now, will you do something else for me?"

She cocked her head as if daring me to bring up the subject of money again. "What?"

"If Gary Carpp wants to meet with you again, will you make it after school so that Barry can join you?"

"I don't understand. Why—"

"There's something a little off about the guy."

"Charmaine, really. I think you're seeing things."

"Just promise me that you won't meet with him alone."

Marietta heaved a pissy sigh. "Fine. I promise. But I assure you. He's done nothing to demonstrate that he's anything but a perfect gentleman."

A shiver trailed down my spine while I imagined Naomi Easley thinking the exact same thing.

Chapter Twenty-Six

"You're a lifesaver," Rox said, grabbing a spoon to dig into the butter pecan ice cream she had asked me to pick up for her after work.

"I'm here to serve." I waited for Rox to waddle past me in her thick socks before putting the turkey sandwich I bought her into the refrigerator. "But promise me that you'll eat at least half of this sandwich. The tryptophan might help you sleep."

She scoffed. "If all this sugar doesn't have any effect, you think a couple of slices of turkey will?"

"It's worth a shot. And speaking of sleep, shouldn't you be in bed?"

"My back is killing me, my heartburn is worse when I lie down, and I'm pretty sure that my hair is now in a permanent state of bed head. So, no, I don't need to be in bed right now."

Leaving the spoon in the ice cream container as if she'd staked her territory, Rox placed her hand over her belly and grimaced.

"What is it?" I asked. "More heartburn?"

"Cramp." She blew out a breath. "There. Gone."

"You're having cramps, too?"

Rox turned that grimace on me as she grabbed her spoon. "Don't even think about suggesting that it's the ice cream. This junk is the only thing that's getting me through the day. Well, that and the movie channel package that Eddie got me so that I wouldn't go completely stir-crazy."

"Gee, pregnancy sounds really fun. I had no idea of the joy I was missing out on."

"You'll probably be like my worst nightmare, Raina. All glowy in her supermodel perfection instead of puking for the first three months."

"Yeah, I want to be like her," I said, trying to keep the bitterness from seeping into my voice, but one glance at Rox told me that I had missed that mark by a mile.

She shook her head. "Sorry, I shouldn't have brought her up. Being a preggo has made me stupid."

I gave my best friend a hug. "If it makes you feel any better, I'd rather be like you." In a heartbeat. "But maybe just puke for one month."

"Oh, trust me." Rox paused for an unladylike belch. "You'd rather be glowy."

"Pretty sure I don't get a vote when it comes right down to it." I was also sure that what I might want was a moot point if Steve didn't want the same thing.

Five minutes after I left Rox's house, I pulled into the Bassett Motor Works lot and parked next to the Jaguar that Georgie had texted me was ready.

Climbing out of the SUV, I glared down at the fancy replacement rim gleaming under the setting sun and thought of how much Chris had once loved his Jag.

After all the money it had cost me over the last sixteen months, I felt no love toward the beast. But I also didn't feel cursed, blocked, misaligned, or otherwise spiritually out of sorts because of its presence in my life.

The Jag had been doing a decent job of getting me where I needed to go.

Most of the time.

With minimal oil drips from a leak that Georgie swore had been fixed.

And it was comfortable to drive.

As long as I didn't think about sitting on any of the bad vibes that Chris had left behind.

"Hiya, Char," Georgie said, emerging from the garage with his dog Rufus trotting behind him. "She should be good to go."

For the amount he expected me to pay before my car left the lot, she had better be purring like a kitten. "Great."

Georgie turned toward the office thirty feet behind us. "Want to settle up so that you can give your granny back her car?"

"Let me ask you something first."

"Shoot."

"Having worked on the Jag a few times ..." Way too many times. "What's your opinion of it?"

"Honestly, she's gettin' a little long in the tooth, but

she's still a beauty." He gave me a lopsided grin while his dog curled into a ball at his feet. "Just a feisty one."

My favorite mechanic could have been describing my mother.

"If you were me, would you be thinking about selling it?"

Pulling a red shop rag from the pocket of his grease-stained overalls, he wiped his hands. "Chow Mein, I woulda done that after we fixed the oil leak, but you gotta realize. You're not gonna get much for it."

"What? You just finished saying it was still a beautiful car."

"She's got almost two hundred thousand miles on her. Nobody who doesn't wanna spend time with her under the hood is gonna want her."

Since my husband didn't want to touch me toward the end, that sounded way too much like a cheap shot. "If I could find a buyer, what do you think I could get for it?"

Georgie thumbed in the direction of the office. "Wanna go inside and find out?"

Less than two minutes later, he scratched his scruffy red beard while frowning at the computer monitor on the counter. "You're not gonna like this."

I was really tired of hearing him say that to me. "Just give it to me straight."

"Best I can find for the same model year is twenty-seven hundred."

"That's it?!"

"Oh, your car wouldn't sell for near that much. Not

with all your miles."

Again, that sounded like a snide remark. "Yes, but it has those new tires and the brake job you just did. That has to count for something."

Georgie stared at the monitor. "It counts toward makin' it a safer car," he muttered while Rufus picked up and whined at the door as if he wanted to escape the tension rising in the office.

"Are you serious?"

He shrugged as if I were asking him a trick question.

"So it's either keep on sinking money into this car or practically give it away."

"Well, I guess you could put it that way."

Swell. "What would you do?"

"If I were you?"

I nodded.

He leaned his elbows on the scarred wooden counter separating us and grinned. "I'd leave her here with my mechanic to sell on consignment."

"Meaning what, exactly."

"I sell her for the best price I can get and keep five percent."

Since I was facing a repair bill in excess of what I'd get out of that deal, I had another idea to float out to my prospective salesman.

I penciled it out on a page in my notebook. "Your five percent would probably be close to one hundred bucks. What if I paid you your commission now and signed the Jag over to you, and whatever you sell it for, you keep."

Georgie stroked his chin. "You wouldn't be trying to

get out of payin' your bill now, would ya?"

Absolutely. "Sell it for a good price and you'd come out ahead."

"Don't think Dad would go for it."

His dad was the "big dog" at Bassett Motors that Junior, affectionately known as Little Dog, worked for. "Want to run it by him?"

Georgie disappeared for two minutes, and then returned, followed by Rufus. "Three hundred to make sure that we turn a profit on this deal."

He stood behind the counter like the football player he used to be, poised to block me as soon as I made a move.

That told me that he expected me to make a counter-offer. "Two hundred."

"Two-twenty-five."

I extended my hand. "Deal."

"Are you sure you don't want something more substantial?" Gram asked fifteen minutes later, while I stood in her kitchen and ate a biscuit left over from last night.

"Nope, I'm on a diet." Lately, a fat-laden carbohydrate diet much like Rox's, which I needed to knock off before my belly got as round as hers.

Gram pursed her lips while she filled her teakettle. "Some diet."

"I know. Fozzie and I will have to go on a long walk tonight."

"Speaking of Fozzie, I assume that you—"

"Cleaned the interior of your car?" I licked my fingers clean and saluted her. "Yes, ma'am, and thanks again for letting me borrow it."

She looked at me over the rim of her trifocals. "I also assume that all's well between you and your mother now."

It was as good as it was going to get. "Yep."

"And there's a plan for doing something with that car outside?"

"I wouldn't call it a plan, but I'll be driving it over to my house tonight."

"And then after that?"

Leaning against her checkerboard counter of blue and white tiles, I stared down at my espadrilles. "I haven't gotten that far."

"It seems like a very nice car. Probably a heckuva lot more reliable than the one that Chris stuck you with."

"About that. I sold it tonight."

Gram's mouth gaped open. "To whom?"

"George Jr." I skipped the part about not making any money on the deal.

"Then you're obviously keeping the Subaru."

"I haven't figured out the details yet."

"What's to figure out? You need a car, and there's a perfectly good one right outside."

"I can't just let her fix me up with a car like some sort of fairy godmother." Much as I could use a sprinkle of pixie dust to make getting through life a little easier.

"Then return it and buy one yourself. Really, I think

you're making this too complicated."

Probably. But the complication was not being able to afford a new car right now.

"I will." Maybe. "After I'm done with—" I clamped my mouth shut before Naomi's name spilled out.

Gram removed her steaming kettle from the burner with more force than necessary. "Don't tell me."

"Okay." Fine with me, since she'd most certainly blab to Steve.

"You're still trying to prove that Naomi's death wasn't an accident."

"Uh…"

Gram waggled a finger at me. "Don't bother denying what you've been up to."

My heart skipped a beat as my mind raced to figure out how much she knew.

"Alice told me how you and Lucille were coming up with some outlandish theories about Robin being the one responsible for her mother's death."

"It was more Lucille's theory than mine, but it wasn't completely—"

"Charmaine Digby, you cannot seriously suspect that girl of harming her own mother."

Not by herself I didn't. Plus, given what I'd found out about the Carpp brothers, I wasn't inclined to totally align myself with Lucille. "I don't know what to think beyond what we talked about last week. Even you and Alice agree that the way Mrs. Easley died was just plain weird."

"That doesn't mean that you should be out there playing detective."

My grandmother had definitely been spending way too much time with Steve.

"I'm not. I'm just doing the basic fact-finding that as a deputy coroner I would do with any unusual death in the county."

As creative fibbing went, I thought that was pretty good until I saw Gram plant her hands on her hips.

"Fact-finding with Lucille's help?" She rolled her eyes. "Facts are typically optional with that one."

"Lucille just happened to offer up an opinion about how she thought that night might have played out."

"I bet she did," Gram said, filling her cup.

"Okay. To play out how that conversation went with her, what do you think led to Naomi Easley being found dead in that bathtub?"

Gram folded her arms while her tea steeped. "I have no idea."

"If you knew that Robin was responsible for her mom's accident at the house two years ago, would you be a little more inclined to think that Lucille wasn't just talking out of her ass?"

"Charmaine!"

"Excuse me, her *bottom* if you prefer."

"Either way, you don't know the story behind that fall Naomi took."

"Not every detail of the story." I locked onto Gram's gaze to let her fill in the rest of the blanks.

She sharply inhaled. "No. You don't mean—"

"Afraid so. Robin practically admitted it."

"To you?"

I nodded.

Gram furrowed her brow. "But that doesn't mean that she was trying to kill her mother, does it?"

"No, but there was obviously some tension there that helps to explain why Naomi kept away from the house after the accident."

"Certainly Stevie had all this information at the time of his investigation."

I doubted that he spent as much time trying to get Robin to open up as I had. "I don't know. We don't talk about that kind of stuff."

"Well, I think you should assume that he would have talked to all the family members, especially Hailey. She's always been very close to her mom." Gram turned to sugar her tea. "I know she's one of the first people I would've wanted to have a chat with."

I couldn't agree more, especially on that last point.

Maybe a ferry ride into Seattle could be arranged for tomorrow.

Chapter Twenty-Seven

Driving onto a Seattle-bound ferry on a sunny Friday afternoon was challenging enough because of the typically long lines of vehicles waiting in the queue.

Today, I hadn't been able find anyone in the county prosecutor's office who could provide me with a legitimate reason to make myself scarce for a few hours, so it had proven to be next to impossible.

Then I remembered the boat captain that I had been researching for Assistant Prosecutor Lisa Arbuckle to call as a witness in a vehicular assault case, and I trotted down to her office because he conveniently lived on the east side of Seattle.

Fortunately, Lisa's door was open, so I gave it a knock.

"Yes?" she answered without sparing me a glance as she clicked away on her computer keyboard.

"Now that I've completed the background checks that you requested, would you like me to start getting some statements?" I scanned the crowded surface of her metal desk and spotted the manila file folder with the case number I had written on the front. It didn't appear to have moved much in the last three days. Considering that she had spent most of this week in court, I hoped her busy schedule could work in my favor.

She finally looked up and huffed in annoyance. "What's that again?"

"I have some time if you'd like me to help with the witness statements."

"Sure." Lisa plucked the folder from her desk and handed it to me like an automaton. "Thanks."

"I could probably line up a couple this afternoon," I said while she frowned at her monitor and made several mouse-clicks.

She waved me away. "Fine. Whenever you can fit them in."

"I can fit in at least one of them just fine today," I muttered, almost running back to my desk.

Less than a minute later, Patsy's steely eyes narrowed as I zipped by her desk. "Heading out somewhere, Charmaine?"

"Witness interviews for Lisa. I should be gone the rest of the day."

Patsy grunted her displeasure, and I didn't care.

"Thank you, Lisa," I thought, bounding down the marble steps while the sheriff's deputy working security focused his attention on me as if I were making a jail-break. Probably because it looked like I was, especially when I hopped into a new car that didn't technically belong to me.

Fortunately, I only had a thirty-minute wait in line to

catch the two-twenty sailing. That gave me plenty of time to leave Eddie a voice message that I might be a couple of hours late. I regretted leaving him short-handed on what was sure to be a busy Friday night, but there was no way I was going to be able to get back before seven. Not with the wretched traffic that I found myself stuck in the minute I pulled away from the Seattle ferry dock.

It wasn't that I hadn't expected the traffic to be bad after three o'clock on a sunny, getaway Friday-type of afternoon. But it was also unseasonably warm and there was some sort of accident up ahead at the entrance of the Interstate 90 freeway, causing me to roll to a stop behind a black diesel pickup.

In my ex-husband's Jaguar with its ineffectual air-conditioning, this was where I'd be faced with a dilemma if I didn't want to start sticking to the leather upholstery. Turn on the fan and suck in asphyxiating diesel fumes, or open the windows to get some air moving and be overcome by fumes.

It took me a second to figure out how to turn on the A/C, but once I felt that cool air hit my face, I smiled and patted the Subaru's steering wheel as if I were giving my dog some love. Not because my mother had been right about how much better I'd feel once I parted ways with the last holdover from my marriage, but because it struck me that I wasn't getting asphyxiated by that truck.

"Yep, much better," I announced, turning up one of my favorite Fleetwood Mac songs on the radio.

But then once I started singing along and the lyrics

"You can go your own way" came out of my mouth, it also hit me that I was enjoying driving this new car a little too much.

I tightened my grip on the steering wheel as I finally merged onto the freeway. "Slow your roll. You're not keeping it," I reminded myself.

By the time I crossed Lake Washington and crawled through traffic on my way north to the Woodinville residence listed in the file next to me, I had poked along so slowly it was after four. If I wanted to have a prayer of catching the six-fifteen ferry back to Port Merritt, I needed to cross the boat captain's interview off of today's list of things to do and focus on the one that might help solve a murder. That required a slight detour and another fifty bumper-to-bumper minutes around the north shore of Lake Washington, where Hailey Kranick Moynahan lived in nearby Lake Forest Park.

Parking the Subaru in front of the pickle-green rambler that the GPS on my phone had led me to, I climbed out and noticed a big, tattooed guy who could have been Little Dog's older brother watching me from the driveway.

But unlike Little Dog, this guy didn't look the least bit happy to see me, especially when he slammed the hood of the vintage Jeep he had been standing behind. "Can I help you?"

I pasted a smile on my face and hoped that the charcoal gray pantsuit I'd worn for the interview to project professionalism would also give me a boost in the confidence department. Because judging by the gravel in this guy's tone, he ate rocks for breakfast.

"Is Hailey here?" I asked, pressing my tote to my side like a shield.

He eyeballed my cheap suit as if he could tell I'd found it on a discount rack. "What's this about?"

I figured I had better respond with something that sounded like it was worth Hailey's time if I wanted to be invited inside the house. "The death of her grandmother."

After a second of consideration, he grunted. "She won't be home until six-thirty. Our daughter has gymnastics tonight."

So much for me catching that ferry. Unless he knew anything that could help me fit some pieces together.

I flashed my badge. "I'm with the Chimacam County coroner's office. Do you mind if I ask you a few questions?"

"About my wife's grandma?"

"I'm mainly looking for background information so that we can properly file the death certificate. Could we talk inside?"

Hailey's husband nodded as if my big fat lie had sounded perfectly reasonable. "Sure," he said, leading the way through the garage to a back door.

Rounding a corner into a family room, where a twelve- or thirteen-year-old boy was lying on a sofa watching some old cartoon, the guy took a wide stance in front of the kid. "Aren't you supposed to be doing your homework?"

The kid grabbed the remote and clicked off the TV. "I was just going to do that."

"Uh-huh." The second we had the room to ourselves, the guy pointed at the sofa for me to sit. "You sure you don't want to wait for Hailey? She's the one you should be talking to."

But she wasn't here.

I parked on the cushion closest to the recliner he had eased himself into and took out my notebook to clue him in about my answer. "It's always good to get other points of view."

I got another grunt, which I took as my cue to proceed. "May I have your name?"

"Nick Moynahan."

"Would you say that you knew Naomi Easley pretty well?"

Nick's shoulder twitched under the charcoal T-shirt that coordinated perfectly with the eagle spreading its dark wings over his forearm. "Well enough, I guess."

"Your wife was living at her grandmother's house when you met, I assume?"

He knit his furry auburn eyebrows, reminding me of Georgie when he wanted me to get to the point. "Yeah."

"Along with her mother?"

Nick nodded.

"It seemed that something happened two years ago that caused Mrs. Easley to feel it was unsafe to stay in the house."

I waited to let him tell me what to ask next by the level of discomfort in his reaction.

Nick clasped his hands, his knuckles white, while his jaw clenched as if he were weighing his options. "You should probably talk to my wife about that."

Undoubtedly, but she wasn't around and he definitely knew something he didn't want to say about it.

"I'll do that. But when this fall happened…" I gave him a little nod of assurance that he wouldn't be divulging any information that I didn't already know. "That's what was in the medic's report, that it was a fall, correct?"

"Yeah," he said after a second of hesitation.

So far, so good. "Did you or your wife get the impression that Mrs. Easley had been drinking that night?"

"She probably had a glass of wine with dinner, if that's what you mean."

"Maybe more than one?"

Nick scowled at me. "I wouldn't know."

Okay. "I imagine Hailey was called that night. Maybe by her mother?"

"Yeah. We got on the next ferry."

"After you got there and had a chance to talk to Hailey's mom, what did you think happened to make Mrs. Easley take that fall?"

He aimed that scowl at me again. "What's this got to do with her death certificate?"

Absolutely nothing, unless the tumble that Naomi took down those stairs was no accident. "I'm just trying to understand what was going on prior to her death."

"You really should be talking to Hailey," Nick said, checking the watch on his thick wrist as if he wished she'd hurry up.

"Yes, but you were there. Did your mother-in-law describe how the accident happened?"

"Not in any detail. I just thought Naomi tripped."

"So no argument that night. Nothing to support a report of an altercation."

Nick clamped his mouth shut for a couple of seconds while his shoulder almost shrugged its way out of its socket. "I don't know."

No, you know stuff you don't want to admit to.

"I assume that's one of the reasons why your wife had to take over all the things that her grandmother had been doing," I said, trying to look understanding. "Probably just made things easier between those two."

"I guess."

Which answered the question about why Hailey had been making monthly treks to her mom's house for the last two years.

"She was in Port Merritt the night her grandmother died, right?"

He nodded.

"Did she call to tell you what happened?"

"Yeah."

"How'd she seem on the phone?"

"Upset," Nick said, raising his gruff voice. "How do you think?"

"I know it's uncomfortable to talk about." Especially for me with the guy sitting five feet away looking like he was itching to toss me out of his house. "But I have a hard time understanding how Mrs. Easley could have drowned. What's the family's take on what happened?"

"That she took way too many pain pills and must've passed out."

Since Nick hadn't given me any reason to doubt his truthfulness, I decided to see what he could tell me about the meeting with the Carpp brothers. "Someone mentioned something about an offer on the house. Do you know if Hailey and her mom went to the condo to talk about that?"

"That wouldn't happen."

"Because your mother-in-law didn't want to discuss that possibility?" Which Robin had made crystal clear to me.

"No, I mean Robin had never been to the condo."

"Ever?"

Nick shook his head. "Hailey thought she was just being stubborn. You know. Mother and daughter crap."

Yeah, I knew all about that particular brand of crap.

"My mother-in-law doesn't leave the house much. Period. But she downright refused to go to Naomi's place."

That blew Lucille's theory out of the water. At least as far as Robin was concerned.

I snapped my notebook shut with the hope that Nick would think that everything else he happened to mention would be off the record. "What's Hailey think about the offer on the house? That big house has got to be worth some money."

"I don't know." He scratched his unshaven cheek. "More than anything, I think she just wishes she could convince Robin to move somewhere closer."

"I'm sure it's tough on her to be the one her mom relies on. Being an hour away by ferry and all."

"Yeah, she talked to a friend in real estate to try to get the ball rolling last month."

I scooted to the edge of my seat. "When was this?"

"The weekend her grandma died. It seemed like a decision had been made, then... Well, everything changed."

I wanted to be sure I understood him. "You mean Robin had made a decision to move?" Because if that was the case, what happened to the arrangement she kept clinging to?

"No. Hailey and I will probably have to drag her mom out of there kicking and screaming."

"I'm sorry, then I don't understand. What changed?"

Shaking his head, a sardonic chuckle escaped Nick's lips. "The old lady changed her mind. Announced she wasn't selling. Pretty much told everyone who kept asking her about it to back off."

I had a feeling that one of them didn't want to take no for an answer.

Chapter Twenty-Eight

After I got home and fed Fozzie, I changed into my bartender's uniform of black jeans and a slightly tight Eddie's Place T-shirt, touched up my makeup, and then dashed over to my Friday night fill-in gig.

"Holy smokes," I muttered while pulling into the one and only parking spot in the crowded lot behind the bowling alley. "What the heck is going on tonight?"

After I apologized for being late, I asked Eddie the same thing when I relieved him behind the bar.

He gave me a satisfied smile. "Isn't it great? And I thought it would be slow tonight because of the football game."

That was why a lot of the local merchants referred to Port Merritt High's home games as "Friday night lights."

"Did the game get cancelled or something?" Because while having the baseball playoffs going on all the flat screens typically enticed Eddie's regulars to stay and have another beer, it didn't usually create a standing-room-only kind of crowd.

"Nope. Since Byron's in town, I invited him and Steve

over for some free pizza. No doubt, word spread." Shifting his gaze toward the sound of raucous laughter at the big center table, Eddie grabbed a plastic tub of dirty dishes. "What the rest of those freeloaders don't realize is that they're getting *one* free pizza."

I looked over and spotted Georgie sitting in between two former teammates who were almost his same size. "How many pies have they ordered?"

"Seven, so the kitchen is hoppin'." Eddie grinned as he set off for the kitchen. "And the beer is flowin'."

The bar made the majority of its profits from the couple dozen beers he had on tap, so I could almost hear the sound of a happy cash register over the din of the crowd.

I could also see Steve coming toward me with an empty pitcher in his hand and a sexy smile on his face.

"Hey, what's the occasion?" I called out to the former high school quarterback over the cheers coming from the guys watching the game. "It looks like most of your offensive line is at that table."

Edging around one of the few unoccupied stools, he leaned against the polished oak railing and handed me the plastic pitcher. "Byron must've said the magic words 'free pizza' to Dog, who called the gang to tell 'em we were meeting up."

"The usual?" I asked, heading over to Steve's favorite brew on tap.

Steve nodded, looking at me as if he liked what he saw, and then he said something I couldn't make out over Springsteen singing about dancing in the dark. "Hold that thought," I shouted.

Seconds later, I slid the foam-topped pitcher toward him. "What?"

He gave me a peck on the lips. "I said nice shirt."

I glanced down at how it was clinging a little too tightly to the roll above my waistband. "I must've had it in the dryer too long. It shrank."

Steve smiled, his eyes dark with carnal intent as he focused on the twin peaks north of my love handles. "Good."

I looked over his shoulder at Byron while Libby grabbed another empty pitcher from their table. "I'm surprised Byron's still in town. I thought he had to get back to work."

"He does. By's catching a redeye late tomorrow, so this is pretty much it for getting together with the guys."

"Hmmm." Since Byron had told me that he wanted to wrap up the negotiations this week, I took his travel plans as an indicator that he'd had to extend his stay because of something happening tomorrow.

"Speaking of work, where've you been?" Steve asked, stepping to one side so that Libby could pass me that pitcher.

"Yeah!" my bar waitress grumbled, punctuating an amber ale fill-up request with a lot more attitude than I was in the mood for.

I shot her a saccharine-sweet smile as I headed for the tap. "My day job."

Steve backed off as if I had fired a warning shot. "Catch you later."

I was counting on it.

Unlike Steve, Libby didn't take the hint and rested her elbows on the bar in a practiced way that revealed some pretty spectacular cleavage. "What do you do again? I didn't really get it from the paper."

I didn't particularly feel like sharing, especially when I spotted Gary Carpp coming in with a kid who looked a lot like the clone I thought I saw at the construction site. "Mainly office work."

"And Marietta Moreau is your mother?" She shook her head, a smug glint in her eyes. "Did you do something to get cut out of the will to have to work two crummy jobs?"

I forced a smile when I passed her the pitcher of ale. "I like to keep busy."

"I can think of more fun ways to keep busy," Libby retorted, adjusting her short black skirt before she sashayed back to the guys' table to treat Little Dog to the next peek down her shirt.

"So can I." But I also didn't want Rox and Eddie to stress about their business. Not when I could easily fill in for a few hours on the weekends. Plus, this watering hole provided me the opportunity to interact with some of the locals that I might not otherwise run into.

I shifted my gaze over to where Gary Carpp and his young doppelganger were heading toward the back to grab a table that had just been vacated.

Spotting one of those opportunities, I grabbed a plastic tub and a bar rag, and fell into step behind them.

"Good evening, gentlemen," I said, clearing away the dirty dishes.

Gary leaned back and smiled at me. "We meet again."

"I know. Small world, huh?" I turned to his look-alike who hadn't demonstrated so much as a flicker of recognition, probably because I had my hair down instead of pulling it back in the ponytail he'd seen two days earlier.

Good, I thought as I wiped down the table.

"It's Charmaine, right?" Gary asked without offering an introduction to the kid I assumed was his son.

Meeting Gary's gaze, I didn't sense anything more menacing than a lack of social graces. "Good memory."

"I didn't realize you worked here."

"I'm just helping out for a while," I said and then paused to give him another chance to make that introduction. When it didn't come, I balanced the tub against my hip. "Can I start you off with a couple of beers?"

"Sure." The kid rattled off the lengthy name of a pale ale I'd never heard of before.

"Let me make sure that I've got that one." I gave him an apologetic smile.

Still nothing but cocky disinterest registered on his face, especially after he cast a glance at my thunder thighs.

I don't care because I've got nothing but professional interest in you. "And of course I've got to take a peek at your ID."

Expelling a stale breath that reeked of cigarettes, he reached for his wallet.

"Take it as a compliment," Gary said after he ordered a Budweiser. "No one asks for my ID anymore."

The kid pulled out his driver's license and flipped it over onto the table like a jerk, making me work for it.

Picking it up, I focused on the thing I wanted to know the most: his name. Sean Davis Carpp.

I did the mental math to determine that Sean was twenty-two and handed the license back to him. "Any relation to the guy who doesn't need to be carded here?"

He gave Gary the same constipated look as my mother whenever she mentioned my "pasty-faced bastard" father. "Yeah."

Okay, his dad was clearly not the hot date Sean wanted to have sitting across from him tonight. "Let me check on that IPA. I'll also grab you a couple of menus."

Libby met me at the bar, where she glanced back at Gary. "Who the heck is the hunk you were talking to?"

No one she should be setting her sights on. "Family friend." My mother liked him, so the characterization was close enough.

"Here," I said seconds later, placing the amber bottle I found in the specialty beer case next to the glass of Budweiser on Libby's tray. "He gets the Bud, and they need menus. Don't know if his wife will be joining them."

Libby groaned. "Figures he'd be married. All the good ones are."

Also the not-so-good ones. Which I couldn't say for sure fit Gary Carpp, but there was still something about him that made the hair at the back of my neck stand on end. Nothing that had set off my lie-dar, but still... Something had told me to beware of the tree guy.

Given what Mike Pollard had told me about some punk at the job site who could get him fired, possibly the tree guy's son, too.

After about fifteen minutes, I had settled into what had become my typical weekend routine of filling drink orders and working the register when I spotted Byron stepping away from the table.

At first, I thought he might be coming over to talk to me since this might be our last chance before he left town. But instead of heading my way, Byron caught Gary's eye and pointed toward the exit.

Seconds later, I stood at the register, where I could see Byron pacing in the front parking lot while Gary seemed to be doing most of the talking. Then with a nod from Byron and a handshake, they retraced their steps back to their tables.

What the heck was that?

While Libby made her rounds at the other side of the bar, I grabbed a pitcher of ice water to give myself an excuse to do some reconnaissance at Byron's table. Because after seven pizzas, those boys should have been awfully thirsty.

"Hiya, Char," Georgie called out as I reached past him to clear out an aluminum pizza pan that looked as if he had licked it clean. "No luck on your car yet, but it's only been a day."

"I didn't expect anything to happen overnight." And really not what I wanted to talk about.

Steve set down his beer glass. "What's going on with your car?"

Georgie puffed out his broad chest. "Technically, it's *my* car now, and I'm selling it."

"What kind of car?" Byron asked while I collected a

mass of used napkins and two empty pitchers.

Since the Jag was now Little Dog's problem, I let him do the explaining and headed over to the Carpp table to see if I could glean any useful information from the far side of the room.

But with father and son watching the game in silence while waiting for their food, I returned to the bar with nothing more than two drink orders and more dirty dishes.

After I poured two glasses of Chardonnay for the ladies at the table behind Gary, I looked up to see Steve sitting at Donna's usual spot at the bar.

"What're you doing here?" I asked him on my way back from making the wine delivery. "Too much testosterone at the table for you?"

Steve grinned. "Thought I'd enjoy the view from over here for a while."

Much as I wanted to believe that was his only motivation, I knew better. "And…"

"And I was curious why you didn't tell me that you sold your car to Dog."

"I didn't see you last night so it wasn't like the subject came up. Anyway, it was pretty much a spur of the moment decision, which is now over and done with."

"So I assume you got here in the new ride."

I nodded. "But it's going back tomorrow."

Steve narrowed his eyes. "What do you mean, it's going back?"

What was confusing about that? "I'm returning it. Maybe they'll have something used that I can afford."

He shook his head. "It's not like returning a pair of shoes. Dealerships don't usually take returns."

I swore under my breath. "I'm stuck with this gift horse of a car?"

"Is that so bad?"

I stabbed my finger at him as I headed for the Friday night regular shaking his empty glass at me. "Said by a guy who doesn't have to deal with this kind of manipulative crap from *his* mother."

After the playoff game ended, Byron, Georgie, and the rest of the team took off, leaving Steve and a pile of cash at the table.

"I don't know if there's enough here to give you much of a tip," he said, counting the bills while I cleared the table.

I was used to his pals not being big tippers. "Don't worry about it."

"Actually, it doesn't even cover the bill." Steve pulled another twenty from his wallet and then handed the wad to me.

"Eddie thanks you, even though the pizza for you and Byron was supposed to be on the house." I looked over at the now-empty back table where Libby was collecting the tip money that Gary Carpp had left her. "Speaking of Byron, what was going on earlier?"

"What do you mean?"

"With him and Gary Carpp having that little meeting outside."

"I didn't notice."

Right. Steve typically didn't miss a thing. "When Byron stepped away for a few minutes, it was to talk in private with the Cascara group rep he's probably been negotiating with."

Steve gave me a pointed look. "No doubt because he didn't want someone like you listening in."

Resenting the fact that Steve had to be right, I pushed him aside so I could wipe down the table. "Tomorrow must be it for getting this deal done that Bryon's been working on, don't you think?"

"I couldn't tell you," Steve said with a little curl of amusement at the corner of his mouth.

"I'm sure he must've mentioned something about it to one of the guys."

The curl extended into a smug grin.

I wanted to wipe that grin off his face with my grungy rag. "Really? You're not going to tell me?"

"Do you tell me everything?"

I set down the tub of dirty dishes I was balancing at my hip and glared at him. "Not everything. Didn't think you want to hear the girl stuff." I couldn't quite bring myself to go so far as Lucille and mention *woman parts.*

Steve hooked his finger in the V of my shirt and gently pulled me close. "Who says I don't?"

If he held me any closer I thought my woman parts might start to melt. "I'm not saying—"

"Good." Steve pressed his lips to mine, giving me a sizzling kiss that he broke off way too soon. "I think you're being paged," he said, turning me to face Libby's scowl.

"Duty calls." I picked up the tub of dishes and started for the bar. "Want to come over later?"

Steve smirked. "Not if you're gonna want to play Twenty Questions."

"I might not even ask you one question. Heck, I might not even talk to you at all!"

"There you go not talking to me again," he said, walking past me toward the door.

"I'm sure we can find something else to do."

"I'm sure we can."

Chapter Twenty-Nine

Three hours later, I was curled up next to Steve while the sci-fi movie he had picked out flickered in the low light of my living room.

I felt warm and safe and loved, with my dog resting his head on my thigh and softly snoring. But that didn't keep my restless brain from niggling at me about what I had witnessed at Eddie's.

Grabbing the remote and jostling Fozzie awake in the process, I paused the movie. "You know when we talked a few nights ago about how the Pollards have received some threats in connection to Ryan testifying?"

Steve hung his head. "I thought you agreed we wouldn't be playing Twenty Questions."

"We're not. There's just something I noticed tonight that I thought I should run by you. As a good citizen," I added like a cherry on top of the conversation I needed if I wanted to have a prayer of sleeping tonight.

"A good citizen." Steve's jaw muscles tightened as he turned to me. "Right."

"Lighten up on the sarcasm and just listen."

He folded his arms, and Fozzie immediately jumped off the sofa as if sensing that trouble was brewing.

"Remember how I was saying that Mike Pollard was concerned that someone might try to get him fired?"

"Yeah."

"What if that someone was Sean Carpp, who I happened to card at Eddie's tonight."

Steve's brow furrowed. "Char—"

"Just hear me out. I'm pretty sure that I saw him at the same job site as Mike. Might even have been on the same crew as Ryan, so what if Sean was involved somehow with the guys you arrested and—"

"No," Steve interjected, shaking his head.

"What do you mean, no?"

"I mean *no*. We aren't going to talk about this again."

"But think about it. Who better to try to get Mike fired than Gary Carpp's punk-ass son?"

Steve's chocolate brown eyes hardened as if they had been flash-frozen. "Unless Mike Pollard would like to talk to me about this himself, I don't want to think about it. Do you know why?"

I was pretty sure it was the same reason he gave me three nights ago. "Because there's nothing you can do about it."

"So will you drop this, please?"

Heaving a sigh, I slumped back on the sofa.

"And do me a favor and stay away from that job site."

The husky quality of his tone informed me that this wasn't solely a professional request. "I'm right about Sean Carpp, aren't I? He's trouble."

"And I don't want you to get on his radar," Steve said, as good as confirming that Sean Carpp had been the one hassling the Pollards.

"I didn't do much more than drive by on the way to see my mother."

"Uh-huh."

Now it was my turn to fold my arms tight to my chest. "You sound like you don't believe me."

"I know you. You're looking—"

"Don't you dare say that I'm looking for trouble again."

Steve grabbed the remote. "Then I guess we're done talking," he said, pointing it at the TV.

"Remember what I said about finding something else to do if you're not gonna talk to me?"

Pausing the movie again, he turned to me with a lop-sided smile. "Yeah?"

"Good luck with that."

Steve set down the remote and wrapped his arm around me. "Did I just hear a challenge?"

I shrugged. "Maybe."

"I'm always up for a good challenge," he said as he lowered his lips to mine.

Stretching out on the sofa to get more comfortable, I pulled him on top of me without breaking the kiss.

After he came up for air, Steve settled on an elbow and grinned down at me. "Something tells me that my luck just changed."

"Now it's time to stop talking." I pulled him back down to claim his mouth and vanquish all thoughts of

Carpps, drownings, ex-husbands, and problem cars from my mind for a few minutes.

I woke up when Steve kissed me good-bye around six and couldn't get back to sleep, so after I took Fozzie on a long walk through the dog park, I hit the shower, where all those thoughts came crashing down on me like a tidal wave.

"One thing at a time," I told myself while I washed my hair.

I didn't have any more leftovers from Chris that I could purge from my life, with the exception of a few of his favorite recipes. That I improved upon, so really they weren't his anymore. And I liked them enough to keep them for now. Mainly because I wasn't willing to spend a dime on that rat bastard's cookbook.

At least I wouldn't have to waste any more money on his car—a comforting thought that put a smile on my face as I luxuriated in the hot water sluicing over me. But once I stepped out of that steamy shower and I met the expectant gaze of the pooch lying in my bathroom doorway, I had to face the stark reality of my situation.

I needed to find another car. Today.

"It needs to be good out in the country," I told Fozzie while I toweled off. "Get good gas mileage. Have plenty of room for you. Not have too many miles on it, and come with a price tag I can afford."

He gently woofed as if he wanted to remind me about the pearly white Subaru parked in my garage.

"I know it's a perfectly nice car, but I can't keep it."

And if the dealership wouldn't take it back, maybe I could find someone else who would.

"Charmaine Digby to see Mr. Ferris," I told Hank when he greeted me in front of the Bayview Estates security gate over an hour later.

Hank gave me a cheery salute as he promptly opened the wrought iron gate. "Have a good day."

As it shut behind me, I could only hope that Mr. Ferris would be more willing to help make this a good day than he sounded when I called to ask if I could come over.

I had just pulled up in front of the house when he opened the front door wearing gray sweats and holding a big ceramic mug of coffee in his hand.

"Want a cup?" he asked, his eyes focused on the zippered envelope in my hand.

I had already downed the majority of the pot I made after Steve left, but if wrapping my hands around a warm mug could make the next few minutes any easier, I was all for it. "Please."

Mr. Ferris pointed to the table. "Make yourself comfortable. Italian roast okay?"

"It's fine."

Sitting in the same chair as the last two times I'd been to his small mansion of a house, I waited for my former biology teacher to join me at the table. But after he placed a steaming ceramic mug next to the zippered envelope in front of me, Mr. Ferris leaned back against the white marble counter as if he were about to deliver a lecture.

"I guess I don't have to ask what's on your mind," he said.

"I can't keep the car." I pushed the plastic envelope to the edge of the table.

"Trust me. As someone who hasn't had much of a vote while your mother replaces everything that isn't up to her exacting standards, I get it."

Thank goodness someone around here did. "I hoped you'd say that because there's a complication. I called the dealership right before I called you. They don't take returns, but I thought my mom might be able to work her magic on them and get her money back."

"Maybe, but this discussion should be between you and her."

I'd had enough discussion with her for one week. "There's nothing else to talk about."

Mr. Ferris smiled at me over the rim of his mug. "I happen to know that your mother doesn't feel that way."

"We've talked. Everything's fine." Or was at least as good as it could be considering the circumstances. "If you'll just explain to her that—"

"You should do that," he said at the same time as I heard a thump that sounded suspiciously like a shoe dropping to the floor above my head.

"She's up?" It wasn't even nine o'clock.

He nodded. "Like I said, this is a matter between you and her."

I could almost feel the other shoe dropping, this time

directly on my head. "Only because she put me in this position. You just finished telling me that you understood how I felt about not getting any say in that car she bought me."

He rolled his eyes. "Believe me. I do. And she and I have had some serious discussions about all this spending she's been doing. Because it's not just *her* financial situation anymore. It's now *ours* together. That's how I know that, while the execution during this rash of spending has left a lot to be desired at times, your mother's heart has been in the right place."

"Says you," I muttered as I reached for my coffee.

Mr. Ferris pressed his warm palm to my shoulder while the click of heels filled the silence between us, and then he handed his coffee mug to the beauty in the olive cigarette pants and buttercream slouch sweater.

"Good morning, my darling." Marietta bent over to give me a quick hug and then slipped into the chair next to me, where she immediately pushed away the envelope. "What a nice surprise."

It wasn't so nice, because this surprise was on me.

"You're up early." And apparently skipped a few steps in her morning routine because her spiky auburn hair was a little damp, and her eyelashes looked almost as sparse as mine.

Her glossy lips curled into a pretty smile, but there seemed to be some strain to hold it, a wavering that told me that she didn't want to be sitting here again anymore than I did. "I never want to miss an opportunity to see my little girl."

Typically, I'd let such an innocuous comment roll off my back like the mother/daughter nicety it was intended to be. But our mother/daughter relationship had always been far from typical, and a sigh escaped my mouth before I could stifle it.

"What?" she demanded. "You have a problem with me calling you that?"

Jeez. This was why I wanted to leave the car with Mr. Ferris so that she and I wouldn't face off with one another as if we were in some sort of pissy cage match.

I took a three-count to mentally reset. "Call me whatever you want. It doesn't matter."

Marietta reached for her coffee. "Sounded like it mattered to me."

Argh! "I'm here because there's a problem. I can't return the car."

She slanted a glance of irritation to the envelope on the table. "Why not? Everything should be in there."

"The dealership doesn't accept returns." I pushed the envelope in her direction. "Of course, they might if you used your Marietta Moreau charm on them."

"I think that might put Renee in a difficult position."

That was more important than the impossible position the two of them had put me in? "That may be a factor in all this, but I can't keep the Subaru for all the reasons we've already talked about."

"I really do get where you're coming from. But I wish you'd reconsider, because I truly hate seeing you in Chris's old car."

"I sold it, so that particular problem has been taken

care of."

Leaning toward me, my mother examined my face. "Other than the fact that you don't appear to be getting enough sleep, I can see that your energy looks better this morning."

I seriously doubted that, but okay.

Settling back in her chair, Marietta smiled with satisfaction. "Good for you for purging yourself of the last vestiges of that cad. I'm very proud of you."

I shouldn't have cared, but a little bubble of pleasure floated to my tongue before I could bat it down. "It was a good decision that you actually helped me make."

"Would you allow me to help you make another one?"

That bubble popped with my brain screaming at me for opening that door for my meddling mother. "Maybe."

"This is one of practicality," she said while the cell phone in my tote bag started ringing. "Do you need to get that?"

"I'll call them back." I just wanted to finally close this topic of conversation.

"Like I was saying, I'd like you to think in terms of practicality. You need a reliable car, and there's one that fits that description parked right outside."

"Mom, we've talked about this."

"Just hear me out." Marietta straightened as if she were steeling herself against the pushback she knew would be heading her way. "I know I haven't always been there for you, but I'm here now and available to you, however you need me."

Oh, it was way too late for her to decide that she

wanted to be a full-time mom. "I appreciate that but—"

"And that includes financially."

No way. "But—"

She raised her hand to silence me and, apparently, my phone, because it suddenly stopped ringing. "Sweetheart, I wish you would stop being so stubborn about money. Half of my estate will be going to you eventually."

"Well, I certainly don't want or expect that to be anytime soon."

"And I don't want anyone to start counting any chickens where I'm concerned, but let me just say that I will be leaving you with a very comfortable nest egg."

Not at the rate she had been spending it. "Fine."

"So the way I would like you to think of that very practical car out there is that it was purchased with some of the money that will be coming your way."

For an actress best known for her physical attributes, she had delivered that line rather convincingly. "Nice try. We both know why you bought it when you did."

"Because your grandmother said you needed a car. Pretty much the same way she mentioned that her old car broke down on the way to her favorite yarn shop a few years ago."

"You bought her that SUV?"

My mother shrugged. "She needed a new car."

Gram hadn't mentioned that little detail when Chris and I flew in for the holidays and she picked us up in a new Honda.

"And if I can do a simple little something to help my mother out after everything she's done for me … Well, it would be selfish of me not to." She waved a manicured hand. "And, naturally, she protested too, but you should have seen the smile on your grandmother's face when she first got behind the wheel."

"But that was an entirely different situation." And Marietta didn't try to use it to gin up some positive publicity.

"I don't see it that way."

Shocker. "You don't owe me anything."

My mother gave me a smile as brittle as the eggshells we had been walking on since she came into the room. "Of course I do. I owe you a mother—or more precisely, a better mother who is here for her daughter. Won't you let me be one?"

She couldn't have knocked the wind out of me more effectively if she had punched me in the solar plexus.

"I promise I won't drag you into Seattle to buy matching dresses like when you were four," she added with a tentative titter.

I used to love our shopping dates in Seattle. Mom and me, along with Gramps because he wouldn't let "Mayhem Moreau" get behind the wheel of his car. "I—"

"But if you'd like to go shopping in Seattle sometime, I'd love it if you'd like to make it a girls' day out."

"That sounds like fun." Or at least had the potential to be if she could contain her urges to turn the day into a mini-publicity tour.

My mother pressed her hand to mine. "Wonderful. Now, about that car. Can we agree that while I may have let some outside factors influence my thinking, I truly was just trying to provide for my family."

"But you need to understand that I don't want you to do that for me."

"I do." She reached for her coffee. "That's why I've discussed the matter with my new financial advisor."

From the twinkle of glee in her eye, I had a feeling there was a lot more to this story. "When did you get a new financial advisor?"

"Thursday night, when I was telling Barry about the offer I got on the house."

I couldn't help but smile at her happy news. "I take it was a good offer."

"Not as good as the counter-offer they accepted last night!" she squealed as my phone began to ring again.

Considering all the months my mother had been trying to unload her Santa Monica estate, this newsflash couldn't have been happier. "Awesome!"

"I know. It's actually so awesome that we've decided to give our children some of their inheritance now."

I studied her face, expecting to see the little tension lines around her eyes or the chin she jutted out when she was trying too hard to sell a story. But all I could see was the blissful glow of true joy. "What?"

"Jason's trying to buy a house," she said while I reached for my phone to shut it up. "Well, he hasn't come out and said as much to Barry, but since we expect that Jason's going to propose fairly soon to that pretty girlfriend of his, I wouldn't be surprised. And I would certainly suspect that they could use the money."

So would I, but the timing of this decision sure felt

fishy.

I was also concerned about the timing of these calls and took a peek at the caller ID to make sure it wasn't Rox or Eddie. It was Lucille, probably calling about some juicy rumor, so I let it go to voice mail.

While Marietta beamed, my stomach churned because never ever had she made good decisions with her money.

"How much are we talking about?" I asked.

"Not a lot. Fourteen thousand now and another fourteen after the New Year." She winked. "Have to be savvy about gift taxes, you know."

Since when was she savvy about any of this stuff? This had to be Barry's influence on her thinking.

"That's a lot of money to me." And interestingly, it added up to the sticker price showing through that envelope.

My former teacher was a lot sneakier than I had given him credit for.

"My darling, do you know how much they paid me for my last movie? It's a drop in the bucket."

Whoa. That must have been some big bucket.

Marietta locked onto my gaze. "So, you see? You really did buy that nice car out there with your own money. As of January first. I just sort of floated you a loan in the meantime."

"That's a *creative* way of looking at it," I said while my phone lit up with another call. *Criminy, Lucille!*

"It was Barry's idea because once the house closes, we're going to have a lot more money than I'll be able to spend anytime soon."

I found that difficult to believe.

"Let me get this so that she'll stop calling." I pressed my phone to my ear. "What?!"

"It's about danged time. I've been calling and calling," Lucille huffed.

"I know. I've been a little busy. What's going on?"

"You need to get your hiney to the cafe. Something's going down!"

Chapter Thirty

I wasn't sure what I would be walking into when I stepped through the front door of Duke's Cafe. Pretty much all the tables were occupied by the regulars who made going out for breakfast a weekend ritual, so that seemed normal.

The same could be said for the hum of friendly chatter, the silver bell jingling behind me, and the mouthwatering aroma of bacon grease assailing my nostrils.

I didn't see anything to clue me into what might be going on until Leland Armistead waved his napkin at me from the nearby table he was sharing with Althea and Mavis.

"Good morning," I said, stepping up to their table, where it appeared they were almost finished with their eggs and pancakes. "How's everyone doing this sunny Saturday?" *Anything going down with you guys?*

"We are very well." Leland's eyes narrowed behind his heavy-framed glasses. "And happy to see you, Miz Charmaine, because there's a curious meetin' goin' on over there." He looked past me. "At least I find it quite curious given our prior conversations."

With syrup on her lips, Althea turned to Mavis sitting next to her. "Are we m-missing a m-meeting or something?"

"No, honey." Mavis patted her sister's hand while shaking her head at Leland. "I think our friend here is trying to make a mountain out of a molehill."

I snuck a peek to check out the molehill, but I didn't see anything more interesting than Arlene, the senior center activity director, meeting with two members of her staff near the side window.

Leland winked at me. "I don't know. Seems to me we've had some interestin' goings-on of late," he said, holding out his cup for a refill from the waitress squeaking in our direction.

As Lucille rounded the table to slosh foul brew into their three cups, she drilled me with a scowl. "You're needed in the kitchen."

Since I didn't know what the heck was going on, I smiled politely and played dumb. Which wasn't a stretch this morning. "Looks like she might put me to work, so I'll stop back to see how you're doing later."

Leland reached for the sugar. "I'm holdin' you to that, Miz Charmaine. Because I don't plan on leavin' anytime soon."

Okay, this clever old dude had to have seen the same thing that Lucille had called me about, so I didn't hesitate to follow her into the kitchen to get up to speed.

Hot on her heels, I waved to Hector Avocato, Duke's long-time weekend manager, behind the grill.

His head turned as we blasted by. "*Querida*, what's the rush? You want some bacon and eggs, or are you still on your diet?"

Like most everyone who worked in this cafe, he knew my habits way too well. "I—"

Lucille grabbed my denim jacket sleeve. "She's a little busy right now."

"Maybe later," I said over my shoulder while she pulled me back to Alice's worktable.

Lucille peered into the restroom near the back door and then eased herself down on the closest stool. "Okay, the coast is clear."

I sat across from her. "What's going on out there? Leland mentioned some sort of a meeting."

Her mouth flattened into a grim line. "If you have to ask, then you didn't get a load of what was going on at table nineteen."

That was the booth in the back corner—farthest from the kitchen and not visible from the main entrance, making it the preferred location in the diner for meetups that required a little privacy. "I didn't get a chance before I was *summoned* in here."

The pucker lines above her coral lips signaled her annoyance. "Missy, you got summoned because you wanted me to let you know when I heard something about that Cascara company."

My thoughts immediately went to Byron since I knew this was his last day in town to try to get that deal done. "Is Byron Thorpe here?"

"What?" Lucille screwed up her face. "No. The son

running the outfit for old man Carpp is here."

Not alone, according to what Leland told me. "Meeting with someone?"

Staring across the table at me, Lucille's mouth pulled into a tight little smirk. "I'll say. Gordon Easley and his wife."

"Whoa." They had to be meeting with one of the Carpps about the sale of the house. Maybe in advance of meeting with Byron.

I needed to get out there, so I peeled off the jacket and stowed my stuff in my locker. "Whose table is that?" I asked while I pulled on a clean apron over my plaid flannel shirt and regretted that I hadn't worn something more waitressy.

"Courtney's." Lucille started walking back toward the dining room. "But they're probably gonna be finishing up soon."

In other words, hurry. "Will you let her know I'm going to take over? Tell her I'm an old friend or something."

With a nod she picked up her pace. "Will do."

Following Lucille out the kitchen door, I headed for the coffee station while Hector watched me through the cutout window.

"Is something going on that I should know about?" he called out to me.

I waved him off as I went by with a coffee carafe en route to the meeting I didn't want to miss. "Don't be silly. I'm just going to help out for a little while."

He chuckled. "Knowing you, help yourself out is probably more like it."

Sometimes, my reputation in this diner wasn't the least bit helpful. But since I had refilled a few thousand coffee cups here over the years, topping off three more shouldn't give anyone reason to look twice.

Although by the arched eyebrows on Gary Carpp's face as he watched me approach, it might have helped my cause if I hadn't been the one to take his drink order last night at Eddie's.

"How many jobs do you have?" Gary asked as he pushed his cup toward the edge of the table for a refill.

I aimed my best customer service smile at him. "Just one unless Duke gets short-handed, then all family members get pressed into service."

"You're related to him too?" Paula Easley tightened her gaze while I poured. "My goodness, what an interesting family you have." She glanced across the table at Gary. "She's also related to Marietta Moreau."

Gary gave me a wink. "So I've heard."

Good grief. I didn't want to be the subject of their conversation.

I had the carafe positioned over Gordon's cup when he shook his head. "No more for me," he said, pressing his hand to his chest.

Paula turned to him. "Are you okay?"

Gordon didn't look okay to me. He had the ashen pallor of a zombie from one of Marietta's old movies, with a bead of sweat trickling down his temple.

He took a long drink of water. "I'm okay. I just had too much coffee."

I'd developed plenty of sour stomachs from sucking

down too many cups of Duke's rotgut brew. I'd even broken out in a sweat on more than one occasion, but I was pretty sure I had never looked like the undead. At least not if I'd followed my usual makeup routine.

He pushed away his plate with the Spanish omelet he had barely touched. "The tomato in this may have been a mistake."

"Would you care for something else?" I asked as Gary's phone started to ring.

Gordon put his hand to his mouth but was unsuccessful in stifling a belch. "Yeah, some antacid."

I couldn't help him there.

Paula moved their two plates toward me while Gary excused himself to take the call. "I think we're done."

Dang! This meeting was breaking up, and I had yet to learn a thing.

I carried their plates to the dirty dish cart on the other side of the thick half wall that separated this section from the main dining room. With no tables within ten feet of it, standing by the cart was the perfect place for Gary to take that call, but the only thing I could hear him say was "One o'clock? See you then."

"Sorry to interrupt," I told him when he shot me an irritated glance.

"No worries."

By the steadying breath he sucked in before striding back to the table, I had a feeling Gary was trying to convince himself not to worry about the brief exchange he'd just had, not me.

I grabbed one of the water pitchers from the stand by

the wall and started following him, but got waylaid by a tourist at the next table holding up an empty glass.

By the time I refilled all their water glasses, Gordon had pushed back from table nineteen.

"Do you think a little more water would help?" I asked him.

Gordon grimaced as he stood. "With a pill I need to take, yes." He looked at his wife. "I'm going to the drug store across the street. Be right back."

"I should get going too." Stepping away from the table, Gary picked up the bill and then squeezed Paula's shoulder. "We'll get this done."

She nodded. "We need to."

I filled her water glass. "Everything okay?"

Paula shook her head. "It will be, one way or the other."

I grabbed a napkin to clean the table, affording me a good look at her face. "I heard about today's meeting with some of the other sellers. The way an old buddy of mine described it, you guys could be sitting on a pile of gold."

She pressed her lips together as if she'd taken a vow of silence on the subject, but not before the corners of her mouth quirked into a little happy dance. "I really don't know—"

"You probably don't come here enough to realize what a small town this is. It's *really* hard to keep a secret. Trust me when I say that there are a bunch of us who can't wait to see what Cascara does with the property." *Please trust me.*

Paula glanced back at the table the water guzzlers were leaving. "Nothing's a done deal yet for *our* property, so..."

I slid onto the seat that Gary had vacated. "But you must be getting close, otherwise I can't imagine that Mrs. Walker would have told me—"

I clamped my mouth shut. "I probably shouldn't repeat it."

Paula's pupils dilated with interest while she schooled her features into a Mona Lisa pose. "You can tell me. I've been talking to the neighbor about this deal for weeks."

She had?

No wonder Paula had wanted to pounce on that banker box like Fozzie on a pork chop when I mentioned that Naomi had listed the house. Paula hadn't wanted anything to screw up this multimillion-dollar deal.

"It was just that the word 'negotiation' was used." Not by Vivian Walker but by Byron, when he asked me not to repeat what I'd heard.

I shrugged as if such big words were beyond my comprehension. "Robin must have had a change of heart, huh? The last time I talked to her she was pretty determined to stay put."

Paula rolled her eyes. "I think her brother is going to have to be a little more persuasive than he has been so far."

"I'm sure it will work out. Really, it's obvious the house is too much for Robin. When my grandmother and I went there to return that box of Naomi's things, we practically had to use a machete to get to the front door,"

I said, dangling that bit of hyperbole in front of Paula to see what reaction I could get.

Mona Lisa's smile stretched with satisfaction. "It's remarkable what can happen over the course of three months."

"Excuse me?"

"It's been three months since Gordon's heart attack."

Paula was telling me this as if it were common knowledge. "I didn't realize..."

She flicked a wrist. "Oh, he's doing fine now that he's not killing himself with that albatross of a house."

I remembered what Gram had said about Gordon helping Naomi with things around the house. I just hadn't realized she had meant Naomi's *old* house at the heart of this development deal.

"So he was handling all the yard work for Robin." And now there was three months' growth of weeds taking over the landscape.

"He did everything for her. No matter how sick it made him." Paula's eyes turned to stone behind her tortoise shell-framed glasses. "But that's over now."

I wasn't sure that I understood. "Because of his health."

Her lips thinned as if she needed to be cautious with her answer. "He needs to take better care of himself."

"Sometimes guys are stubborn and need our help with that," I said, watching her carefully.

Closing her eyes for a second, she blew out a shaky breath. "Indeed."

"He's lucky to have you looking out for him."

Paula hesitated as if she wanted nothing to do with where this conversation was heading. "He's doing much better. The heart attack was really just a warning."

"That some changes needed to be made, right?"

Color flooded into her cheeks, telling me that I'd just hit a bull's-eye. "Most of them small ones, like an aspirin regimen."

I could think of one great big one that Paula must have had a hand in. "But getting your husband out from under all the maintenance work of that house must have been huge."

She looked over her shoulder like she wanted to get out from under Duke's roof and meet Gordon outside. "It's been very good for him to relax on the weekends instead of coming down here to play handyman."

"I bet selling the house to get rid of that stress all together would be even better."

"That's certainly my hope."

I had a sinking feeling that it was more than just a hope, and with Gordon Easley coming toward the table, I had time for just one last gasp at getting to the truth.

"How many weeks ago did you start talking to Mrs. Walker about this deal that's in the works?" I asked with enough volume for Gordon as well as Courtney taking an order three tables over to hear.

"What are you two talking about?" he asked, standing next to his wife while opening a small box of antacid.

"Nothing." Paula set his water glass in front of him. "Take your pill and let's go."

"Actually, I was just asking your wife about this development deal that she and some of your mother's old neighbors have been involved in." I looked across the table and noticed all the color draining from Paula's face. "Because she said the discussions have been going on for several weeks, which really surprised me since it hasn't even been a month since your mother's funeral."

Gordon held the pill to his lips. "Going on for two weeks, maybe. Not that it's any of your business."

"Well, sir, as a deputy coroner of the county where your mom died under some mysterious circumstances, it kind of is my business."

Whether anyone else in my department would agree with me might be debatable, but he didn't know that. "So if your wife was aware of an offer on your mom's house prior to her death, that seems like information that the investigating officer should have had."

Gordon turned to his wife. "What is she talking about? We didn't get an offer until last week."

"Take your pill," she bit out, the cords in her neck strained above the collar of her lavender pullover. "We can talk in the car."

Not so fast. "Gary Carpp was seen with his brother at your mother's condo the afternoon of her death."

Gordon took the pill but frowned as if it were leaving a bitter taste in his mouth.

"I heard from one of your mom's old neighbors that the Cascara guys approached them around that same date, so it only makes sense that they went to her condo to make her an offer."

Gordon stared down at Paula. "You knew about this?"

She swallowed. "I didn't want to bother you with it in case it all fell apart."

"Bother me?" he repeated, raising his voice.

"So I went to make sure—"

"You went there?!"

"Just to facilitate the meeting," Paula softly insisted.

Gordon's head looked like it might explode. "Facilitate!"

Her eyes glittered with tears. "I—"

"You knew my mother wasn't ready to sell." Gordon slammed his palms to the table. "She couldn't have made that more clear the last time you brought it up."

"No!" Paula slapped the table with equal volume. "She was more than willing to kill you with the burden of that wretched house, but I wasn't."

His breath shuddered. "What are you saying?"

Paula gazed up at her husband with tears trickling down her cheeks. "It was to protect our future together. Gordy, she was never going to sell. Your mother would have let Robin live there rent-free until the last dollar of her savings was gone. Then we'd have to support the two of them!" She wiped her eyes with her coffee-stained napkin. "You never would've been able to retire."

"No, honey." Gordon dropped down onto the bench seat behind Paula as if his legs could no longer support his weight. "She was almost to the point where she would've had no choice but to sell the house. My mother knew it too. She even mentioned having another talk with Robin about moving closer to Hailey. All *you* had to do was wait a few weeks, and Mom would've finally been ready to say yes to the next offer."

While Paula buried her head in her hands, Lucille peeked around the corner. "Everything okay?"

Hardly.

I stepped away from the table and set Gordon's water glass in front of him in case his stomach was churning with as much acid as mine was. "I'll be right back."

"I need to call Steve," I whispered in Lucille's ear on my way to the kitchen to grab my phone. "Keep an eye on things for a couple of minutes, okay? And let's shut down this section."

She puffed out her chest as if I had appointed her my junior deputy. "Then something really did go down."

Yep. Way down.

Chapter Thirty-One

I was hiding out in the kitchen with a plate of scrambled eggs to avoid Leland's probing questions about why Steve had joined the "meeting" going on in the corner.

Leland was a clever man. And since he was the one who called in the "murder" of his neighbor, I had no doubt that he could figure out that I had made today's call.

I just wished the detective I had called would now do a little communicating of his own, because the suspense was killing me.

I was thinking that I might have to channel my nervous energy into baking (and eating) some cookies when I looked up and saw Steve striding in my direction.

"What's happening out there?" I asked, envying his calm demeanor.

He stole a slice of cold toast from my plate and took a bite. "I'm going to take Paula and Gordon to the station for a chat."

"They were pretty talkative right before I called you."

Nodding, Steve swallowed. "I'm sure they were, but I

think we all realized that this isn't the private setting that our discussion will require."

"Got it. I do want you to know that I called as soon as it became obvious that Paula was responsible for Naomi Easley's death."

Steve smiled, his gaze locked on mine. "I don't know how you managed to get her talking the way you did. I probably don't want to know. But you done good."

"Wow." I wanted to bask for a moment in his praise, my insides turning as gooey as a block of chocolate over a flame. "Thanks."

Then he abruptly focused on some message on his cell phone. "It's probably going to be a few hours before I can get to the hospital, so I'll meet you there later if you're itching to get going."

If Steve had wanted to dole out some mental whiplash, he was doing a great job of it. "What?"

"Eddie texted fifteen minutes ago." Steve grinned. "With some interesting spelling for 'hospital,' so Pop must've been pretty excited that it's finally baby time."

Holy smokes!

I checked my phone for messages. Nothing. Then it dinged with a text from Rox to both Donna and me.

Just checking in at hospital. No need to rush over, but it looks like Jr will be coming out to play today!

I leapt out of my seat and wrapped my arms around Steve. "It's baby time!"

✳

Four hours later, Steve found me pacing the corridor of the third-floor birthing center, the same thing I'd been doing since arriving at the hospital around noon.

The waiting area at the end of the hall had been crowded with Rox and Eddie's family members as well as some nervous parents of a young mother who had been in labor since early this morning. In need of a private place to talk, I pulled Steve back into the empty elevator he had arrived on and punched the button for the first floor.

"How are you?" I asked after I gave him a proper kiss during the only moment of privacy we might be able to claim for the next few hours.

Steve put his arm around my shoulder. "Tired. If I'd known we were gonna have a confession *and* baby doubleheader today, I never would have agreed to finishing that movie last night."

I elbowed him. "That was your idea."

"Maybe," he said, taking my hand as we stepped onto the first floor. "Where we going? Cafeteria?"

Not my destination of choice because I was hoping to go for a walk in the mid-afternoon sunshine, but since he was following the scent of burgers wafting from the cafeteria grill, I was up for another shot of caffeine.

Sitting at a table in the far corner away from some uniformed employees on break, I waited until Steve picked up his burger and fries and joined me to do a little grilling of my own.

"So?" I asked, stealing one of his shoestring fries while he added ketchup to his burger. "Did Paula Easley give you the whole story of what happened that day?"

"Yep. Probably one of the fastest confessions I ever got. Like she wanted to get it over with before her husband had another heart attack."

"What'd you think of her confession?"

"That she's in a lot of trouble."

"Who'd you talk to in my department for charges?"

"Ben," Steve said with his mouth full.

I waited for him to finish chewing. "And?"

Steve looked at me over his burger. "We're charging her with murder one. Might be a little dicey to prove since there's no conclusive evidence. But we got it in her own words how she helped her mother-in-law into the tub after crushing enough of those pills into her wine to make her pass out, so…"

"Sounds like a strong-enough case to me," I said while he took another bite.

He locked on my gaze while he chewed. "Are you going to try the case as well as solve it?"

"No, smart ass. But I can put two and two together, and see when someone is desperate to hide something."

"And I suppose this math occurred while you just *happened* to be helping out at Duke's this morning."

I stole another one of his fries. "Exactly."

He smirked. "Uh-huh."

"So what happens next?"

"That's up to the judge at her arraignment. Won't be until next week sometime." Steve glanced at his watch. "She should be on her way to County by now. Shouldn't this kid have happened by now, too?"

"You're asking me? I don't know any more about it than you do."

I checked my phone for messages. Other than a frenzied text from Donna, who wouldn't be able to get here until after her last appointment at five, nothing.

I smiled across the table at Steve. "It's kind of exciting though, isn't it? The big day is finally here."

Stuffing his face, he nodded, focusing on his food.

Okay, maybe that was a typical guy reaction. Given his recent editorial comments about the downside of parenthood, maybe I should have expected as much.

I probably had enough of a flutter of excitement in my gut for the two of us despite the coffee acid bath I was giving those restless butterflies.

After he finished his burger, I noticed Steve searching my face. "What?" I asked.

"Are you doing okay?"

"It's just been a long, weird day, and it's not over yet."

He took my hand and we headed back upstairs to the waiting area, where a beaming Eddie was in the hallway with both sets of parents and some siblings outside of Rox's room.

I rushed to join them. "Do we have a baby?"

Eddie grinned. "We have a baby. Alexander David. Seven pounds, eight ounces. Twenty inches long. And with a set of lungs on him that you wouldn't believe."

Steve shook his hand. "Congratulations, Pop. How's Rox?"

"Great. Tired but absolutely great," Eddie said, opening the door to her room. "And she's ready to have you come in if you'd like to meet our little guy."

Standing at the foot of Rox's bed, I waved to my best friend while everyone washed their hands to take a turn holding the baby. "Considering you just pushed a little human out of your body, you look awesome."

Her room had low light with the curtains drawn, but Rox glowed with joy as she watched her mother holding her first grandbaby. "Char, you're a wonderful liar. Now, wash up so that you can hold him."

Those butterflies in my tummy took a swan dive as I stepped to the sink behind me and turned on the hot water.

What was my problem? I'd been looking forward to holding this baby since the first day I found out I was going to be an auntie. But the closer the sleeping little bundle being passed from arm to arm got to me, the faster my heart pounded.

"Are you ready?" Erica, Rox's younger sister, asked, carefully supporting the baby's head to make the transfer.

Hot tears seared my eye sockets as I took Alexander David Fiske into my arms. "Hello, Alex. I'm your auntie Char." *And you feel so impossibly good.* "Want to meet Uncle Steve?" I asked, passing the baby to the great guy on my left who was supposed to be immune to the charm of little babies, but he had a sappy grin on his face.

Then I completely lost it when baby Alex latched onto Steve's finger. "Excuse me a minute," I blubbered, escaping into the hallway with the ache in my heart bubbling north to lodge in my throat.

"What's wrong with you?" Steve asked when he

wrapped his arms around me seconds later. "You've been waiting to hold that baby for months."

"You don't want a baby," I sobbed into the shoulder seam of his black polo shirt.

"Who said?"

He started to stroke my back, and I pushed him away. "You did!"

Steve leveled his gaze at me. "I never said that."

"You said as much on numerous occasions." Okay. Maybe only two, but I felt indignant about having to wipe my nose on my shirtsleeve and wasn't in the mood to provide him an entirely accurate count.

He ducked into the public restroom behind him and handed me some tissue. "I may have pointed out the sleepless hours that Eddie and Rox have ahead of them, but I never would have said that I don't want a baby."

Walking away from him to salvage a little of my dignity, I blew my nose.

Steve stepped up behind me, radiating so much heat as he pulled me close that the cork I'd used to bottle my tears melted.

He gently turned me and wiped away my tears with the pad of his thumb. "We haven't really talked about this, but it kinda seems like now's the right time for it, if you're ready."

Was Steve asking me if I was ready to have THE TALK about having children together?

Oh, heck no!

Steve laced his fingers with mine. "Would you like to have a baby?"

Yes. "Someday."

He pulled me a little closer. "Maybe when you meet the right guy?"

I nodded while I desperately prayed I wouldn't start ugly crying.

"Maybe with someone who couldn't love you more even though you make me crazy sometimes."

Staring into a sea of molten chocolate, I wondered if my brain was short-circuiting because I seemed to have lost my ability to speak.

Steve cocked his head. "It's your turn to say something."

I cleared the clog of emotion from my throat. "So tell me again. Do you want a baby?"

"I do."

"With me, I mean."

He grimaced. "Who else would I mean?"

I threw my arms around his neck. "I love you too."

THE END

ABOUT THE AUTHOR

Wendy Delaney writes fun-filled cozy mysteries and is the award-winning author of the Working Stiffs Mystery series. A long-time member of Mystery Writers of America, she's a Food Network addict and pastry chef wannabe. When she's not killing off story people she can be found on her treadmill, working off the calories from her latest culinary adventure.

Wendy lives in the Seattle area with the love of her life and is a proud grandma. For book news please visit her website at www.wendydelaney.com, email her at wendy@wendydelaney.com, and connect with her on Facebook at www.facebook.com/wendy.delaney.908.

Printed in Great Britain
by Amazon